# THE TRAVELLER

Victor Kelleher was born in London but moved to Central Africa at the age of fifteen. He spent most of the following twenty years there and in South Africa, working at various jobs, studying, and teaching. After three years in New Zealand, he moved to Australia in 1976 and is now Associate Professor of English at the University of New England. He is the author of the novels *The Beast of Heaven* (UQP, 1984), winner of the Australian Science Fiction Achievement Award, and *Voices from the River* (1979), as well as six highly acclaimed novels for children. His forthcoming novel, "Em's Story", set in Africa, will be published by UQP in 1988.

**by the same author:**

*Voices from the River* (novel)
*Forbidden Paths of Thual* (children's novel)
*The Hunting of Shadroth* (children's novel)
*Master of the Grove* (children's novel)
*The Beast of Heaven* (novel)
*Green Piper* (children's novel)
*Taronga* (children's novel)

# THE TRAVELLER

STORIES OF TWO CONTINENTS

# VICTOR KELLEHER

University of Queensland Press
ST LUCIA • LONDON • NEW YORK

First published 1983 under the title *Africa and After*
by University of Queensland Press
Box 42, St Lucia, Queensland, Australia
Reprinted 1987

© Victor Kelleher 1983

This book is copyright. Apart from any fair dealing for the
purposes of private study, research, criticism or review, as
permitted under the Copyright Act, no part may be reproduced
by any process without written permission. Enquiries should
be made to the publisher.

Typeset by University of Queensland Press
Printed in Australia by The Book Printer, Melbourne

Distributed in the UK and Europe by University of Queensland Press
Dunhams Lane, Letchworth, Herts. SG6 1LF England

Distributed in the USA and Canada by University of Queensland Press
250 Commercial Street, Manchester, NH 03101 USA

**Cataloguing in Publication Data**

*National Library of Australia*

Kelleher, Victor, 1939- .
   The traveller: stories of two continents

   I. Title. II. Title: Africa and after.

A823'.3

*British Library* (data available)

*Library of Congress*

ISBN 0 7022 2103 1

For Allen and Eileen

# Contents

Acknowledgments  *ix*

**Part I**

The Road  *3*
The Oldest Africa  *20*
Only a Journey  *29*
The Jackal Fence  *53*
A Nehru Shirt  *68*
The Empty Room  *78*
Chiba & Son  *88*

**Part II**

Refugees  *109*

**Part III**

The Traveller  *129*
Flash  *140*
Quaker Wedding  *150*
Hobbies  *160*
Secret Life  *172*
Three Faces of Terry Couzens  *178*
Reflections  *206*

# Acknowledgments

Some of these stories have appeared before: "The Road", "Only a Journey", "The Empty Room", and "Chiba & Son" in *Landfall* (New Zealand); "The Oldest Africa" in *Islands* (New Zealand); "The Jackal Fence" in *Communiqué* (South Africa); "The Traveller", "Quaker Wedding" and "A Nehru Shirt" in *Westerly*; "Refugees" in *Overland*; "Flash" in *inprint*. "The Road", "Only a Journey", and "The Empty Room" have appeared in book form in *Introduction 6* (London: Faber & Faber, 1977).

# Part I

# The Road

We never did have a son. I used to tell myself it was just bad luck, one of those things you have no control over. My wife, when she considers the matter at all, still regards it in that way. But more and more in recent years, I've come to see it as a kind of judgment. It is almost as if the child has been taken away from me. Thinking of him, now, I find it hard to realize he has never existed. I can visualize him perfectly, not as a vague shadow, longed and waited for, but as a real person, a silent young man, lost somewhere in the past. It's that idea, the irresistible sense of loss, which is hardest to come to terms with. Increasingly, when I'm alone, I find myself searching back through old memories, especially through the years spent in Africa, as though I expected to find him there, to rescue him from some half-forgotten event. The whole exercise, of course, is pointless — it is irrational and, inevitably, reveals nothing. Not a trace of him. For always, no matter how carefully I sift the past, I am drawn back to the same futile recollection: a picture not of him, but of myself, at the age of eighteen, standing late one afternoon at the side of a dirt road in Central Africa.

That picture, at least, is not imaginary. The road was real enough: dusty and badly corrugated, it lay to the east of the main north-south highway, close to the Lake, in what is now called Malawi. And I did once stand beside it, waiting for a lift. At the time I was hitch-hiking home to Lusaka, after three months of aimless wandering in East Africa. I had been dropped on that particular section of the road by a police patrol, shortly after midday. Much later that afternoon I was still stranded there: for five hours there had been no southbound traffic. It is that late part of the day, almost the evening, which I recall most vividly, which keeps recurring whenever I think of the child — like the answer to some other question, one I have never asked — the time and the place so clear in my mind that I can still feel what it was like to be there.

The heat of the day had passed and I had left the shelter of the bush and was standing on the dusty verge of the highway. I can remember how still it was, how deserted. In the tired yellow light, the shadows of the trees lay sprawled across the dust at my feet. The bush, everywhere, was quiet and unmoving. Behind me, back from the road, raised slightly above the beaten earth clearing, was an Indian trading store built of plastered mud brick, with a tin roof and a covered front verandah. The setting sun was shining directly on to the verandah, picking out the few larger items displayed there — the black tin trunks, the multi-coloured pressed cardboard suitcases, an old bicycle tied to one of the supporting roof pillars by a piece of white sisal string.

I too was facing into the sun, beginning by then to feel anxious about where I should spend the night. A hundred yards back along the road was a huge sandstone boulder, much higher than any of the surrounding trees. I walked over to it, left my light rucksack and canvas water bottle in the long grass, and scrambled to the top. Over to the east were the vast reaches of Lake Malawi: from the shoreline, less than half a mile from where I sat, it stretched out into the evening, its waters shining black, untouched by wind. Much closer, between me and the Lake, was a cluster of African huts. To the north, I could see at least three miles along the road. But there was no sign of a car, no tell-tale coils of dust; just the unbroken thread of brown dirt, streaked with shadow, curving away through the darkening green of the bush. I waited there, perched on the top of that rock, feeling lonely and isolated, until the sun had fallen to a point just above the horizon; then I slithered down and, for the first time that day, approached the store.

That in itself was not an easy thing to do. In those days a young white man born and educated in Africa was not supposed to ask a non-European for help, and as I climbed the five mud steps which led up to the open verandah I felt distinctly uncomfortable — not so much vain or proud as unsure of myself. Below me, the ground was already in darkness, but inside the store it was neither wholly night nor day, the last rays of the sun, entering through the door and windows, cutting narrow corridors of light across the shadows. I was met by the usual smell of paraffin and stale bread; a treadle sewing machine stood beside the door; on either side the walls were lined with shelves filled with cheap cotton cloth and tinned food. A short fat Indian, middle-aged, with a pock-marked face, stepped into the light.

"Is there anywhere around here I can spend the night?" I asked.

He shrugged his shoulders and I saw immediately that there was nothing of the unctuous Asian shopkeeper about him.

"We have no place here," he said. He looked and sounded completely unconcerned.

"No police station? No farms nearby?" I asked.

"There is nothing," he said, spreading both palms on the wooden counter as though to emphasize the finality of the answer.

"And your house . . . " I began. But it was too embarrassing even in that rapidly failing light.

He shrugged once again, not even bothering to answer.

"Here then," I said more firmly, indicating the shadowy room in which we stood.

"The law forbids it," he said. "Nobody can sleep in a store where food is kept." He paused. "It is the British law," he said meaningfully.

There was no mistaking either the tone or the significance of that last remark and I turned towards the door. The world had grown visibly darker: only the top edge of the sun was still showing through the trees. But to my surprise he called me back.

"There is the compound, near the Lake," he said.

I didn't understand at first.

"The African compound," he repeated, "down near the Lake."

His tone, as before, was flat and non-committal, but I knew precisely what he meant. He wasn't making a serious suggestion; he was taunting me. And for the first time in two or three hours I ceased to feel either anxious or embarrassed.

In recent years I must have re-enacted a hundred times or more what followed, though the bare events in themselves are ordinary enough. It's hard to say what keeps drawing me back to them. Partly, perhaps, the notion of an unborn child, the persistent belief in my own lost fatherhood. But also a desire for reassurance. It is peculiarly comforting to find that I can recapture completely the last fading moments of that day. Later that night and the following morning everything becomes increasingly blurred, but those moments at least are clear. Now, years later, when I think of that Indian storekeeper's attitude, I can still feel the upsurge of indignation hardening immediately into resolution — a resolution so unexpected, so divorced from my limited background and experience, that it continues to amaze me.

Walking back to the counter I said, "Why didn't you tell me that at first?"

He did not answer and by then it was impossible to see his face clearly: but I like to think that the way he suddenly leaned away from the counter was an indication of surprise.

"Do you sell spirits?" I asked.

"I have no licence," he said.

"Yes, but do you sell them?" I persisted.

He reached into one of the shelves behind him and produced a large bottle of gin. "Sometimes I make gifts," he said tentatively.

"To the Africans in the compound down there?"

"Yes."

"And how much are your gifts?"

Again he shrugged. "I am not a rich man," he said.

Quickly, before he could change his mind, I paid him more than the bottle was worth and left the store.

Outside the dusk had deepened almost into night, leaving barely enough light to locate the path behind the store. I found it at last, after stumbling around in the bush for several minutes, and followed it as it wound between the shadowy shapes of trees. I was still too angry to think clearly about what I was doing and before I could collect my thoughts I had reached the village. As I stepped between the first two mud huts the dogs scented me. I caught a glimpse of a fire surrounded by a small group of people and then I was too busy swinging my rucksack, trying to keep the dogs from my heels, to notice anything else. They backed off only when an African ran over, swearing and brandishing a stick.

As soon as the barking had stopped he stepped back several paces, respectfully, waiting for me to speak. He was a short, slight man, of indeterminate age in the near darkness.

"Who is the chief here?" I asked.

"He is there, *Bwana*," he said, pointing to the group by the fire. I went over to them. There were twenty or more people in the clearing between the huts, but only four men seated or crouched by the fire, all of them elderly, one of them very old. He alone remained seated, wrapped in a blanket, grey-haired, his eyes disfigured with cataracts. There were murmurs of greeting. The man who had beaten off the dogs came forward. I could see now that he was young, not more than twenty-five, with a round very black face. He was indescribably ragged, dressed in cast-off baggy trousers and a short-sleeved shirt, both of them many sizes too large.

"They don't speak English, *Bwana*," he said quietly. "I worked for the government, three years."

I looked at the row of old faces.

"Ask them . . ." I said, and hesitated.

"Is the *Bwana*'s car broken?" he asked, trying to be helpful.

"I have no car," I said, and at the same time took the gin from my rucksack and placed it on the warm earth beside the fire.

I expected them to talk among themselves for some time, but almost immediately the very old man rose slowly and, bending towards me, beat the fingers of one hand gently in the palm of the other in a gesture of thanks. Then he signed to the young man who disappeared into the shadows for a few minutes, reappearing with a collection of tin mugs and chipped enamel bowls. The gin was divided equally into six portions and, one after the other, each of us drank his share. The old chief began the ritual. Raising his bowl carefully, he drained it in two or three heavy gulps. The strong liquor made him wrinkle up his whole face, but after the first shock he nodded contentedly to himself several times. While the others drank, he produced a dirty old rag from somewhere in the folds of the blanket and carefully wiped each of his rheumy, reddened eyes.

Afterwards, they talked quietly for a few minutes. I couldn't understand them, but it was obvious they were discussing me. When they stopped, the young man again went into the shadows. I had squatted down on my rucksack and now I moved up closer to the fire, not for the heat, but to get some protection from the mosquitoes. We sat there together, silently. Occasionally, the old chief looked across at me, pointed to the empty bottle, and nodded with satisfaction. At the end of about an hour, they all stood up, again made the gesture of thanks, beating the fingers of one hand into the palm of the other, and filed off towards the shadowy outline of the huts.

Apart from a few thin dogs, curled up just outside the circle of the fire, I was alone. The only sound was the usual night clatter of insects. Silent, in the huts all around me, the whole village slept. A light breeze had sprung up and I could smell the Lake nearby — a kind of damp earth smell, slightly musty. When I listened very hard, I thought I could hear the light slap of water, of small waves washing in among the reeds. I settled myself more comfortably, wedging the rucksack behind my back for support. There was enough wood to keep the fire going for several hours yet and I took it that I had been left there for the night. The prospect didn't really bother me. I was hungry, but I understood the reluctance of the old men to spoil the slight effect of the alcohol with food. Lying back, looking up at the stark outline of Orion pinioned somewhere in the blackness of space, I thought of the huge sandstone rock, where I had sat watching the road, and of the Indian store, empty now and in complete darkness, its two front windows staring sightlessly out onto the deserted clearing. He had said tauntingly, "There is the compound, near the Lake," knowing that for people like me that was no alternative. And suddenly, unexpectedly, for the first time that evening, I felt happy about what I had done. Not just content: positively happy — sitting there alone, yet ringed around with all those warm and silent sleepers.

It was then that the ragged young African came back.

"Please for the *Bwana* to come," he said.

I gathered up my things and followed him into the darkness. One of the dogs, lying near by, lurched to its feet, round-backed, almost skeletally thin, and hurried across our path. He walked to the edge of the village and stopped, out of sight of the fire, in front of a small round hut, made of packed mud and with an untidy, overhanging thatched roof. He pulled aside what I later discovered was a rusty length of corrugated iron and revealed a low doorway.

"For the *Bwana*," he said simply.

I had to bend low to enter the hut. As soon as I was inside, he replaced the makeshift door and I heard his footsteps as he walked away. I never saw him again after that.

It was pitch black in there. I had expected it to smell stale and dirty, but it was merely warm and airless. Crouching down, I groped blindly forward and touched someone's foot. Oddly enough, I don't think I was very surprised: I must have realized almost immediately that for the old man the question of hospitality went beyond the idea of mere shelter, and that the person in the hut with me was a woman. I felt the ground around her and found she was lying on a woven reed mat, little more than three feet wide. There seemed to be no other floor-covering in there, just the bare stamped earth all around. Crawling foward, I lay down beside her, using my rucksack as a pillow. She had not moved or made a sound, but I could hear her quick shallow breathing and knew she was awake. Lying so close to her, I could detect the faint wood-smoke smell of her skin. I reached toward her, brushing her arm with my hand, and touched the warm soft cotton of her dress. Slowly, I slid my hand up towards her breast and then down to the curve of her stomach and onto her thigh. She still did not move, her whole body strangely passive.

"Did the old chief make you come here?" I said. But she did not understand.

*"Bwana?"* she said questioningly, her voice little more than a murmur in the stillness of the hut.

For some reason the intervening years have eroded the actual sound of that voice, made it peculiarly indistinct. Whenever I try to listen to it, to picture the person behind it, I automatically imagine a fully mature, even motherly, woman lying there in the darkness beside me. Yet at the time it seemed so different: what I heard or thought I heard was the voice of a very young girl, virtually a child, unsure of herself, too frightened even to protest. She said nothing else, just that one word: but it was enough. I withdrew my hand and turned away, rolling over to the very edge of the rush mat, as far from her as I could get.

For some time after that I too lay quite still, listening and waiting. Only when her breathing became deep and regular did I allow myself to relax. But even then I did not change my position; and I was still clutching the edge of the thin rush mat when I eventually fell asleep.

I like to think that is important — my being turned away from her at the moment of sleep. It shows that although I may have been impulsive or unrealistic, I was not hypocritical. Consciously, at least, I acted in good faith, with no other guide in all that darkness but her young voice. Regardless of whatever else happened in the course of the night, nothing can alter that fact.

What did happen is that I awoke, minutes or perhaps hours later. The time doesn't really matter. The main thing is that it was too late, because at the actual moment of waking I was already leaning over her, touching her, and by then there was no going back. I neither have nor had any recollection of moving towards her or of pulling up the loose-fitting cotton dress. All I can remember clearly is the wood-smoke smell of her skin, pungent now, seeming to fill the hut, and the quick wakeful rush of her breath against my face — nothing else until I was lying beside her once again, listening to the rustle of the mat as she pulled her dress down.

It was probably then that I really began to wonder what she looked like. I spoke to her again, asking her whether she was all right, but she did not answer. Outside, the wind had risen, sweeping in from the Lake, stirring the thatch above our heads and rattling the makeshift door. Somewhere, in one of the nearby huts, a baby began to cry, quietly at first, and then more loudly, the sound going on and on, the same wretched wail repeated endlessly. Nobody else seemed to hear it or to be bothered by it; it was as though everyone had stolen away from the village in the night, leaving me alone with the child. I cupped both hands over my ears, blocking out the sound, and eventually, after what felt like hours, I managed to go back to sleep.

When I awoke again the sun had risen and she had gone: light was spilling through the open doorway on to the mat where she had slept. I crawled across the dirt floor and looked out, half expecting to see her, but the village was almost deserted, the women already in the fields, the men probably fishing on the Lake. I shouldered my rucksack and water bottle and walked between the rows of huts to the spot where the fire had been the night before.

The old man was sitting there alone, crouched on a low wooden stool in the morning sun. As soon as he saw me he brought both hands up to his forehead in greeting and then called to someone behind him. A tall, large-boned African woman, no longer very young, came out of one of the huts carrying a round black pot. She neither spoke nor looked at me. Kneeling beside the ring of stones she began preparing a fire to heat the food she had brought. As she brushed aside the cold ash, revealing the still live coals beneath, liberating the warm smell of wood-smoke, it suddenly occurred to me, with a sense of shock, that this could be her, the girl in the hut, this large gaunt woman, so passive and silent, obeying without protest the orders of the old man. I had no positive proof that the girl had been young — only the one word and my own impression to judge by; and I could have been mistaken about the voice, misled by the darkness.

The woman was breaking small sticks and placing them carefully on the hot coals. I crouched down beside her and said sharply, "What are you doing?"

She looked up, startled. *"Bwana?"* she said nervously.

It was the same word, the same tone of voice. But there, in the bright morning light, it was impossible to match the two sounds, the one made by the visible, ageing face, the other spoken out of the darkness.

I stood up. The old man was sitting with his eyes closed, dozing in the early warmth. Without disturbing him, I made my way over to the eastern edge of the village, to where several paths curved away through the undergrowth in the direction of the Lake. The one I followed led me down to a small sandy bay, flanked on either side by heavy floating weed. There was still a breeze blowing, scuffing the tops of the low waves, making them sparkle as they flowed in towards the shore. Further out, the deep water looked shiny black against the flat-bottomed clouds which lined the horizon.

I had not washed or changed for the last twenty-four hours and I undressed and waded out through the small waves. The water felt cold at that time of the morning, but not unpleasant. When it reached almost to my armpits, I ducked right under, sinking down until I was sitting on the sandy floor, with fragments of mouldering leaf and half-rotted weed, kicked up by my feet, whirling past my face in the brackish water. As I came up, a single egret, very white and clear-winged, glided down over my head and landed on the grassy bank above the bay. To the left of the bird, on the path I had just taken, a small group of African children, dressed in ragged shorts and old cotton singlets, was watching me silently.

They ran away when I swam back to the shore. Left to myself I sat down for a few minutes on the warm sandy beach. But I was in a hurry now; I did not want to spend another night near the village. As soon as I was reasonably dry, I took from my rucksack the one change of clothes I carried with me, dressed quickly, and climbed up toward the huts.

The woman had gone and the old man was alone once again. He smiled, showing a row of worn even teeth, and indicated the pot resting in the warm ashes of the fire. Inside, there was a ball of *nshima* — boiled maize meal, cooked stiff and dry, almost like crumbly white bread — and two small fishes, deep-bodied talapia taken from the Lake. I had had no food since the previous lunchtime, but I ate only enough to take the edge off my hunger. Then I thanked the old man, using the triple handshake he was familiar with, and hurried away toward the road.

The Indian was standing on the open verandah, but as soon as he saw me he turned and re-entered the store. I, too, did not want to be watched and so I walked a short way along the road and waited in the shade of a tall overhanging tree. Within half an hour an old Bedford truck came down the road and stopped beside me in a swirl of powdery dust. There were three African labourers crouched on the back and another one in the cab, on the passenger side. I heard the driver, a European in his late thirties, say to him, "Get out and let the *Bwana* get in." The African opened the door and swung himself on to the back, grinning affably at me as he did so. I climbed in and sat down in his place, the seat still warm from his body.

"Where're you making for?" the driver asked.

"For Lusaka."

"Hell," he said. "I'm pushing through to Blantyre. Best I can do is drop you off on the Fort Jameson road."

He put the truck in gear and pulled away. Above the road noise and the roar of the engine he half-shouted, "How'd you get here at this time of the morning?"

I glanced over my shoulder, through the back window, at the Africans crouched behind the cab, trying to keep out of the wind. One of them had tied a dirty piece of cotton cloth around his face as a protection against the billowing dust.

"I slept out," I lied. "In the bush."

"Well you chose the right time of year for it," he said. "Just the same, it's a bit risky. There're still leopard around here, you know; not a lot, but still some."

I nodded. The truck rattled on over the uneven surface.

"Mind you," he went on, "leopards aren't the only problem." He jerked his thumb over his shoulder at the four men in the back. "If the truth be told, they're probably your biggest risk."

They were huddled together behind us, placid and

unmoving, their faces expressionless in the rush of air.

"Oh, you can't judge them by the way they look now," he said. "They seem peaceful enough. But think about the way they treat their dogs and their cattle — or their women come to that, especially when they've had a drink. They're like animals then; you really see them as they are."

"All of them?" I said.

It was at that moment, I think, that the feeling of bitterness and impatience began to well up.

"Enough of them."

"Enough for what?"

He laughed. "Enough to make it risky sleeping out alone in the bush miles from anywhere," he said, and laughed again.

There was nothing new or startling in what he said. Most of the farmers and policemen and government officials who had given me lifts over the previous three months had expressed similar ideas. But on that particular morning I didn't want to listen any longer to their faded arguments. It wasn't simply a case of objecting to a racist attitude; that would have been relatively straightforward. No, there were other more personal and involved reasons for that sudden upsurge of bitter impatience; a whole series of them, starting with the painful realization that I had only gone to the village in the first place because I had felt outraged, insulted by an Indian storekeeper, and ending with a group of children standing by the lakeside, silent and fearful. It becomes increasingly difficult to be more explicit than that; because I don't pretend to understand the situation completely, not any more. Yet at the time the whole thing seemed clear enough — so clear that it was impossible to go on sitting there, beside the man, in the comparative comfort of the truck, for a hundred miles or more.

"Would you drop me off here?" I said loudly.

"What was that?" he asked, surprised.

"Would you stop? I want to get out."

He glanced across at me, puzzled. "Is it something I said?" he asked.

"Not really. I just want to get out."

"Look, I'm sorry . . . " he began, but I had already reached over, switched off the ignition, and pulled out the key.

"What the hell are you doing!" he shouted.

He braked sharply and the old truck slithered across the road and came to an abrupt stop. One of the Africans in the back let out a short, almost childlike, cry of alarm. I jumped out of the cab, tossed the key on to the seat, and slammed the door. He shouted something else, but I wasn't really listening. I had already decided what had to be done, and even before the truck had started up again I was hurrying back along the road.

It was a long walk, three miles or more through the bright, increasingly hot morning. I saw nobody on the way. The wind from the Lake had died completely and the bush was as quiet as the woman in the hut, the umbrella tops of the thorn trees poised in the still air, the tall yellow grass already fallen sideways in the early summer heat. The store, when I finally reached it, looked like a derelict citadel, with its grimy plaster walls and corroded tin roof. I crossed the clearing, going first to the tap at the side of the building, to fill my water bottle for what lay ahead; then I climbed the five mud steps for the second time.

The bicycle, an old black Rudge, was still there, tied to the pillar with the sisal string. I didn't want to go inside the store again, so I called from the verandah, "How much do you want for the bicycle?"

He came to the door, as reserved and apparently unconcerned as he had been on the previous evening.

"Four pounds," he said.

I took out four of the six pounds I had left and gave them to him. He folded them neatly and slid them into the top pocket of his shirt.

"Another gift?" he asked drily, with just a trace of sarcasm.

But his attitude didn't bother me any more; whatever anger I may have felt was no longer directed at him.

"No, not a gift," I said, purposely misunderstanding. "I gave them my gift last night. This is more of a debt."

As I spoke, a small Indian child, dressed only in a light smock, crept out of the store and stood behind him, peering round at me with large dark eyes.

"They are simple people," he said seriously. "The other gift was enough, without this."

"The bicycle is for myself," I said.

He frowned, not understanding.

"But there is no town near here, nowhere to cycle to; Lilongwe is over a hundred miles away."

The child encircled one of his legs with both bare arms — the smooth young skin, with its slight sheen, a soft diluted brown against the white of the cloth.

"Yes, I know," I said.

It took me only a few minutes to prepare for the journey. I lifted the bicycle off the verandah and tied my rucksack firmly to the carrier with the piece of sisal string. The water bottle I slung across my back. He picked the child up as I set off. I rode slowly out of the shade, into the sun, bumping across the bare clearing. At the road I turned southwards, pedalling laboriously, trying to avoid the worst ruts, forcing those thick old-fashioned tyres through the deep clinging dust of the little-used road.

I can picture the scene with perfect clarity: the fierce, late morning sunlight; the surrounding bush, sunk in drought, almost watchful in its stillness, the glaring white furrow of the road, walled in on either side by tufted grasses. I can even recapture my own physical sensations: the strain of pushing the pedals down, one after the other; the prickle of sweat across my back; the cool patch on my side, where the water bottle had slid round. But that is all. The rest, what I was thinking and feeling, what it was that ultimately drove me to make that pointless gesture, is largely lost, buried in the darkness of the village — for it is there that the most personal memories first begin to fade and blur. And all that remains is a jumble of unconnected ideas: remorse, anger, determination, bitterness, disappointment, futility — mere words.

To some extent it's like watching another person ride away, unsure of where he's going and why; no longer myself that I picture. I'm often tempted to think of him in that way, as somebody else, young, fair-haired, idealistic, silly in many respects; somebody I was once close to but have grown away from now. I still know a lot about him, plenty of facts. He could be impulsive, venturing into areas of life he hadn't yet learned to cope with; he could be careless, emptying his seed thoughtlessly into the body of an unknown woman, with what results I shall never know; and he was peculiarly prone to regret. But all of that is observed from the outside, as it were: the person himself has become a kind of stranger.

Which, as always and for a variety of reasons, brings me back to the point at which I began: to my son — unborn, unknown, lost; the thwarted memory a kind of judgment.

# The Oldest Africa

He was just eighteen when he left England for Africa. Like a child he imagined dangerous, even violent adventures in which he would star. But above all he wondered about Africa itself. Lying in bed at night he translated his half-formed thoughts into words and asked the darkness, "What is Africa? What does it mean? What will I discover?"

His ship sailed from Southampton near the end of the English summer. On the first night at sea a group of white Rhodesians, celebrating their departure for home, got drunk and smashed up the bar when the steward tried to close it. During that voyage he also encountered the equatorial sun which, in one searing afternoon, left him with painful blisters across the back and chest. At the time, however, neither incident troubled him particularly.

Cape Town, his first physical contact with the continent, looked bright and warm, swept clean by a moderate south-easter. Except for the dark mill-like structures around the docks and the ragged black dock workers, everything was tinged with the yellow of the sun and the blue-grey of Table Mountain. But, for him, nothing of what he saw had the peculiar stamp of Africa about it.

He took the train north and trundled slowly across the parched Karroo to Kimberley, then on to Mafeking and through the scrub of Botswana, and finally across the broad savannah lands of Rhodesia and Zambia and up to the Congo border. Again, it was not what he had expected. The savannah, especially, with its neatly spaced trees and waving yellow grass, reminded him a little of untended parkland. Secretly, he suspected that he had envisaged humid jungles; but later, when he visited the Congo basin, those too disappointed him. And yet the questions, the conviction that something would happen and suddenly enable him to see it, discover what he had come for, all these ideas stayed with him.

Mufulira, the copper mining town he was to live and work in, was as different from his imaginings as everything else. What surprised him most was its dullness — street after street of square, red-brick houses, each with a bare earth drive. He lived in the men's single quarters (small, semi-detached bungalows shaded by mango trees) and had a man servant of his own, an African who washed and cleaned for him and woke him each morning in time for work. The front window of the bungalow, which ran right across the whole building, wasn't really a window at all, but a gauze screen. It was like living outdoors, only cooler. In the rainy season he put an extra blanket on his bed and at night, when it stormed, he often lay on his back, with the fine spray from the screen settling gently on his face.

During that first year he spent an increasing amount of time at the Mine Club, playing tennis or billiards, sitting on the broad verandahs talking late into the night. In one sense, the Club became Africa — its gardens where hydrangeas and roses wilted in the heat or drought, its colonial architecture, its silent black waiters, immaculate in white coat and fez, moving softly, on bare feet, across the polished red floors. From being a place of refuge, somewhere to escape to after tedious afternoons in the wages office, it became a kind of habit. It was as natural to go there as it was to work or to sleep. So that gradually, without his consciously accepting the fact, the unknown Africa, the land, the people, began to concern him less.

But then, one afternoon in late winter, he was riding in a car with a friend who was driving across to Ndola to play tennis. On the way back a small bush buck suddenly sprang on to the road in front of them. They were travelling too fast and, as they swerved to avoid it, the car skidded off the road, rolled over three times, and crashed sideways into a tree. He was shaken but almost completely unhurt, and in the first glad realization that he was still alive, he pulled himself up through the window space and sat, dazed and relieved, on the side of the overturned vehicle. He was surrounded for several seconds by swirls of dust. As these subsided, he became aware of the afternoon whine of insects. There was no breeze. The trees and grass, dried almost grey by the drought, were faintly touched with the green of fresh shoots. In the distance, just back from the road, an African boy was standing, watching him. As the boy began to run towards him, he dropped back into the car and found the driver, dead, blood trickling from one ear, where his head had been smashed against the post between the two side windows.

He went less often to the Club after that. Sometimes, at weekends, he drove to a border town, called Mocambo, because of the coloured prostitutes who worked at the hotels there. After one of these visits, walking back to the Zambian side of the border in the early hours of a Sunday morning, he came across a huge figure stretched out in the middle of the dirt road. It was one of the Afrikaans miners, a giant of a man, lying quite still, his head haloed by a pool of blood which shone black and silver in the moonlight. He managed to rouse the man and help him back to the car where he sprawled in the back seat, only semi-conscious, still bleeding profusely. At the hospital the doctor cut away the stiff black hair at the back of the man's head and revealed a severed artery which pumped out a thin stream of blood at precisely regular intervals. "You would have died," the doctor said, "if you'd been left there on the road." Afterwards, lying in a hospital bed, the big man said, "Old Piet won't forget this favour. Old Piet won't forget it." He never found out who had attacked the man.

In his own case it was different. He had approached one of the coloured dancers and been savagely warned off by an Irish miner. Later that night, while he was walking back along the same stretch of road, a car came past him slowly and stopped a short distance ahead; two men climbed out and stood barring his way. He did not actually remember being beaten.

There must have been a storm while he was unconscious, because when he came to he was sodden and cold, lying in thick wet mud at the side of the road, out of sight of anyone who may have walked back to the Zambian border. The night was dark and still, loud with insects. With the one eye that was not puffed and closed, he looked slowly round at the tall black shapes of the surrounding trees; he could find no sign of dawn. Staggering and sometimes crawling, he made his way back to his car and drove once again to the hospital, where they cleaned and stitched his battered face.

He did not leave his single quarters for two weeks. Three times a day his servant collected food from the mine mess. Most of the time he lay on his bed, pondering about Africa and his life there or watching the gecko which hunted across the ceiling above his head. Once it attacked a large grey night moth and, in the struggle, lost its foothold and fell on to his bare leg. It froze there, watching him with tiny eyes, its sides palpitating urgently. He could feel its cool suckered feet on his skin. Gently, taking it between both palms, he stood up on the bed and placed it back on the ceiling. But it disappeared after that.

As soon as his face was completely healed he went again to the Club. It was a Saturday night and the whole building was crowded, with black waiters hurrying between the tables, their white jackets streaked with sweat. Halfway through the evening the man called Piet approached him. "I never forget a favour," he said again, and walked quickly down the screened verandah to the public bar. There was a commotion inside, and he re-emerged dragging the Irishman by the shirt collar. The man was helpless in the powerful grip. Before he could regain his balance, Piet hit him in the face, knocking him down amongst the crowded tables. He stood up slowly, but Piet stepped forward and hit him again. People were dodging out of the way, stepping over the fallen chairs. He did not get up this time and Piet began dragging him to his feet and knocking him down, in an almost systematic way. The beating seemed to go on for a long time. The manager, a short, grey-haired, slightly corpulent Englishman, kept shouting, "You bloody Dutch barbarian!" But nobody interfered. The waiters stood strangely grouped together, their fezes making a red blotch against the faded cream of the wall. Afterwards, the manager said to the crowd at large, "How can I run a place like this with only black labour to back me up."

At the end of the month he left his post at the mine and moved to a much smaller mining town fifty miles to the north. His new single quarters were built on an earth slope, bare except for a few tall, rough-barked, leafless trees. After work on wet afternoons, he would sit on his open verandah watching the muddy streams of rain water scouring ragged channels in the earth. The seasonal rains were heavy and lasted longer than usual that year. Sometimes, at night, he dreamed of waking wet and cold in the mud.

When the rains stopped he began playing tennis again. He also began taking out a young school teacher who worked at the local government school. He had forgotten his earlier visions of thrilling adventures, but the old questions about Africa, still not fully answered, were as persistent as they had ever been. Increasingly, now, they troubled him. Walking to the tennis courts in the late afternoon, he would glance across at the African compound, with its rusty lean-tos and crumbling mud huts, and remember a similar compound near Mufulira, where he had seen a heap of dead dogs in the street, shot during one of the rabies scares; or going home at night, after visiting the school teacher, he would hear something move in the long grass beside the road, a snake or a rat, and suddenly sense the strangeness of the shrill darkness.

Coming home late on one such night, he found the door of his quarters open. He picked up a large stone and approached the doorway quietly, but the flat was already empty: his clothes, the rugs on the floor, even his mattress had been stolen.

After he had called the police, he stood at one end of the empty bedroom and looked round at the bare, slightly discoloured cream walls. There were no curtains at the window and the bare bulb in the middle of the room cast his shadow, black and threatening, on to the earth slope outside. He knew there was little the police could do, that his belongings had probably been smuggled across the border already.

Two days later, however, the police rang him at the mine and asked him to come down to the station. They said they had arrested his house servant on suspicion.

When he arrived, a young assistant inspector took him through to a back room, where the servant, a man called

Johannes, was being questioned. He was an overweight, oldish African, with grizzled hair and an unhealthy, expressionless face. Now, he looked older than usual, sitting round-shouldered on a plain wood mahogany chair, staring vacantly at a heap of clothing on the table in front of him. A thick-set, very dark-skinned African sergeant was standing next to him.

"Would you like to identify some of this stuff?" the assistant inspector asked.

As he walked across to the table, he noticed for the first time that the only window in the room was barred. It took him only a moment to sort through the clothing. There were two of his shirts in the heap, old faded shirts, with worn cuffs and collars.

"These are mine," he said, but he was trying to remember whether he had seen them recently or whether they had been pilfered weeks before.

The assistant inspector said, "Ask him where he got them."

The sergeant rattled out something in Bemba. Johannes, looking down at the floor, shook his head slowly and replied in a murmur, his thick, slightly mottled lips barely moving.

"He says the *Bwana* gave them to him," the sergeant said.

He knew he should make up his mind quickly, because it meant the difference between large scale robbery and petty theft. The assistant inspector was looking at him questioningly, waiting for him to speak. With an effort, he pictured to himself the room and the cupboard, but both were empty and dark, and he was standing outside, a heavy stone in his hand.

"No, they were stolen," he said. It was technically correct, but he never fully understood why he said it. Afterwards it seemed too late to retract.

"Tell him he's lying," the assistant inspector said.

"Ask him whether he stole them from the *Bwana*."

The sergeant spoke sharply in Bemba, and again Johannes shook his head. Without warning, the sergeant hit him hard on the side of the face with the heel of his hand. He lurched sideways, almost falling off the chair, having to clutch at the table to keep his balance. His face, after the first spasm of pain and surprise, remained expressionless.

"It's best to leave this kind of thing to their own people," the young assistant inspector said confidentially. "And it does save a lot of work if we can get a confession. We're short-handed up here, you know."

To the sergeant he said, "Ask him again."

Through the barred window, he could see the stamped earth yard at the back of the station. A small black child, quite naked, was playing in the dust. After the second blow he walked hurriedly out of the room, along the cool dark passage, and out into the fierce sunlight. The assistant inspector followed him to the car.

"I'm afraid there's not much chance of getting any of the good stuff back," he said. "He'll have passed all that on by now. But at least he won't get away scot-free. I'll give you a ring when he talks."

He rang the mine again early that afternoon.

"The sergeant's just taken down a full confession," he said. "It should be quite straightforward from now on."

Suddenly, he remembered watching Johannes picking small striped caterpillars from the bark of the trees that grew around his single quarters — shuffling from tree to tree, dropping the tiny creatures, still alive, into a tin can. When he had asked him what he wanted them for, he had said, "For eating, *Bwana*." The two old shirts, he was sure now, had been missing for some time.

"Thank you," he said, and replaced the receiver. This time the future was partially decided for him.

Only a few days later there was massive flooding in the underground workings and the mine had to close down. He was offered a job in one of the other towns, but he chose to go back to England. The questions he had asked himself, lying alone in the dark two years earlier, had finally been answered, and there seemed little reason for staying.

In the last weeks he thought a great deal about those two years. He also pictured to himself the journey back: the train crawling across the wide plateau; the rust-streaked sides of the ship cutting into the black waters of the Atlantic. He wished that he could return to a time as well as a place, that the journey could somehow rewind the skein of his experience and leave him a boy again, merely dreaming about the Africa he had yet to discover.

He remembered how his father had said laughingly, "You're following in the footsteps of Livingstone. He travelled to Central Africa." There was, he now realized, a certain macabre humour in the comparison. Both he and the great explorer had followed boyish dreams to their source — Livingstone, finding trust and fellowship in the darkest, most savage parts of the continent; and he, so many years later, rediscovering the oldest Africa of them all. There, he supposed, lay the difference.

# *Only a Journey*

We did not know him until that Sunday morning in late summer when he knocked tentatively on the kitchen door and we went out and found him standing quietly on the stamped earth drive. We had been expecting the knock and someone vaguely like him for two days, ever since we had told the African servant next door that we needed somebody to work in the house. But he was certainly not what we had hoped to see. I think it was his dirtiness which put us off most of all: not just a general grubbiness, but a thick grime of brown dust smeared into his skin and hair and clothes, only his shoes free of it, showing startlingly black and polished beneath the filthy khaki trousers.

None of us spoke for a minute, and as my father won't talk about him any more I shall never know for sure what he intended to say. But while we were waiting for him to ask what I, in my father's place, just on the strength of that first impression, would certainly have refused — in the long silence in which he seemed incapable of saying anything, too withdrawn and confused to speak with the promptness that Europeans usually expect — my mother suddenly stepped forward and held out her hand for his identity papers. He handed them to her nervously and she flicked rapidly through them, finally looking at us instead of giving them back.

"His name's Simon Mapeni," she said. "He's come all the way from Nyasaland."

It was not just what she said, nor the way she said it, but what we all, with a little catch of guilt, immediately

29

guessed it meant. And it was then that he found the courage to speak in his faltering English.

"I want a job, *Bwana*," he said.

So that right from the start we knew something about him, something about the long four hundred mile journey from Nyasaland to Lusaka, something about the very day he had set out; deducing it all from the thick ingrained dust of the slow miles and from the single pair of trousers and the shirt, both unfit to be worn yet unchanged for weeks, and from the shining pair of shoes, unblemished, wrapped protectively in brown paper to within sight of this house — probably the only parcel he had had to carry along the whole length of the road. It was not much to know; but it was enough to get him the job. The rest came later, pieced together slowly; not intentionally, because we didn't think he was important enough to warrant a round-table discussion. Perhaps if we had known that he had come with a kind of purpose we might have taken a more positive interest in him — especially if we had guessed how fully we were going to frustrate that purpose. But fortunately and inevitably we had no idea about any of that.

Almost everything about the unwitnessed years before that day is still hazy, only the missionary standing out clearly. I have never met him and never will, and yet he's vaguely familiar because of all the other men of his type that I have seen or talked to. They are usually American, quiet and fixed in their needs and desires, doggedly witnessing for their Jehovah, erecting their watchtowers all over the vast African plateau brick by varicoloured brick. But they are not just preachers: it seems to be a rule of their creed that they should also have a steady job and actually be a part of the community they dwell in. Which means that this one must have arrived in that tiny lakeside village in Nyasaland, still wearing his trilby hat and dark suit and carrying the black leather case that held his Bible, and somehow found a means of employment over and above all the preaching and instruction he was there to give. I don't quite know how he did it, but he must have been partly successful. At least in Simon's case he was wholly successful, because he not only taught him to write and to spell and read his Bible: he also baptized him and renamed him with staggering aptness, and going one gigantic step beyond even that, managed to convince him utterly; so utterly that he had felt confident about tearing him away from his family and his village, uprooting him and sending him off, without money, to a strange land and people to do at least one job of which he had absolutely no conception. It must have been like a modern laying on of hands, except that in this case if we had chosen to turn him away he may not have had much dust to shake from his feet, but he would have created a mountain that Mohammed himself could not have budged if he had tried to dislodge what was clinging to the rest of him.

Fortunately for us we took him in and without realizing it avoided whatever curse his mentor might have drawn from the black book and called down upon us. But a week later, nothing, not even a direct knowledge of that curse itself — if it had ever existed — could have stopped my father exploding with irritation. My mother did well to restrain him from throwing Simon bodily out of the house. As it was he merely shouted a lot and finally sacked him.

To be honest, I was surprised my father lasted as long as seven days. I think that like my mother and like me he was a little staggered by the magnitude of that trip: it was not simply the distance, at least four and maybe as many as five hundred miles, nor the fact of his utter poverty, nor the ranged hills of dust that his heels must have flicked up day after day; but all those things taken together and seen in the light of this small, fine-boned, almost demure figure — smooth brown-skinned beneath the grime, young yet of indeterminate age — who moved silently and ineffectively about the house. Yet once my father had recovered from the puzzlement of that, he finally saw clearly what none of us had been able to ignore altogether throughout that week of patient fruitless teaching: the inescapable fact that, now he had arrived, Simon was nothing more than a burden around the house, completely ineffective, gazing mystified at the kitchen and everything in it, his own position included.

As sorry as we had been for him at the beginning, when the door closed on him for the first time we all felt more than a little relieved, sure that whoever knocked on the door on Monday or Tuesday could not possibly be any worse. Except that there never was another knock on that door, because when we stumbled out into the kitchen on Monday morning Simon was still there, waiting foolishly for us as though all he had to do was say good morning to earn his wage; and no amount of shouting seemed to convince him otherwise. It was as if it had occurred to him when he had stood dirty and penniless at our door and we had taken him in that this was partly, at least the beginning of, what he had come here for, and that to leave us would betray not just his own good fortune, but the whole greater idea of fortune and fate as such.

He really was, for the first time in our presence, exactly like his namesake, and my father's most ferocious efforts could drive him no further away than the steps of his *kaia* at the bottom of the garden. If we had but known it, even that was a kind of victory, because from then on it was all that we could do to get him outside the kitchen door. And locking it did not help us either: no matter what time of the day we arrived home, he would be squatting there on his hams, waiting patiently for us to let him in. Eventually, on Tuesday night, in desperation, my father locked him out of his *kaia*, but by midnight my mother was so upset about it that she went out and let him in herself.

That was the second time she interceded for him. It was also a kind of thin end of the wedge, because after that it was inevitable that we should take him back, and on Thursday we officially let him into the kitchen that he had never really left. Even so, my father needed a lot of talking down. He had a theory which he shared with a large percentage of the European population in East and Central Africa that Africans as a race admire strength and that once you give in to them they take you for a weakling. He said that now we had taken Simon back he would be good for nothing. Of course my mother's obvious answer to that was that he was useless anyway, so we had little to lose. But he was still uneasy and he finally gave in only on the condition that we should give Simon nothing but his keep until he genuinely began to earn a wage. So he stayed on, and confounded both my father's theory and the general one that people will do anything for money: because throughout all those penniless weeks and those long pointless hours in which we became not his stern employers but his desperate teachers, he remained the same bland smiling person.

They were funny weeks, a kind of stalemate in their way, with my father calm and furious by turns — I forget how many times he did sack him eventually. Nothing could drive him away: in spite of all that he could not grasp or learn about his job, he seemed to know, with a faithful and unwavering certainty that could not have occurred to us then, that he ultimately belonged where he had been sent and had arrived; knew it, moreover, with only faint consciousness and therefore all the more completely. Which is why the dismissals fluttered past him almost unnoticed — except perhaps for that one time when my mother went out alone and unlocked the *kaia*.

Anyway, after that first abortive attempt, the dismissals weren't really dismissals at all; we were all reluctantly fond of him by then and they were more my father's way of working off the frustration that we all felt as our teaching and instruction consistently achieved nothing. Simon seemed to live in another sphere from us, with anything as mildly mundane as housework precluded; there was even something a little unreal about him, which is why I know that that missionary must have settled in Nyasaland years ago and why I'm sure that he taught not only the men and women but also the tiny children who would normally have spent their time playing in the mud at the lake's edge.

But then, after two months, something seemed to click magically into place. Overnight, apparently, he became a changed person. It was as if his mind, which had never really left the mud hut and ring of fire-blackened stones which to him was home, finally agreed to follow him along that long road, achieving in an instant what his body had had to accomplish so painfully. So that from then on the roles were reversed and it was more than we could do to answer all his questions; he took on everything at once and still looked around for things to do. My father, ironically, was more genuinely pleased than any of us: he took to shouting just as proudly and loudly about Simon as he ever had at or against him. At long last it began to look as though the whole episode was going to end satisfactorily.

But for Simon it was only a beginning, because at the end of that third month he received his first wages.

I was still at high school at the time and always first

home in the afternoons, so I suppose I had more chance than anybody else of noticing what was happening. Not that I really used my chance. Usually I cycled straight up to the kitchen door and went in for something to eat or drink and saw him sitting there by the stove in his hours off, quietly studying his Bible. I actually seem to remember that particular Monday at the beginning of the fourth month, the way the kitchen was unexpectedly empty when I arrived, and how he came in only seconds later with his Bible under his arm and the big trilby hat sitting straight on his head. In itself there was nothing unusual about it, because most Africans in that part of the world like hats. What was unusual was the fact that it only happened the once, as though it were only some kind of trial run. After that the hat was put away with the shoes which, in his eyes, had already passed with honours their critical test.

It was the same, exactly one month later, with the black leather Bible case, new and shining, brought ostentatiously into the kitchen I had only just entered, the worn Bible drawn carefully out of its future resting place, not this time to be read so much as to complete the experiment — his habitual broad grin, that since his success had replaced the shy half-smile, turned towards me for the final approbation of what he already knew with near certainty to be right and necessary. And then the Bible case too disappeared and he was back by the stove in the afternoons, scanning and plotting his course across the chart of the Scriptures.

By that stage I had guessed something was happening and for a time I was waiting for the next move. Though as it turned out I had a long wait because a black suit is far more expensive than a hat or a briefcase, and when he did finally walk into the kitchen, his bare feet very brown against the wide black turn-ups, I was just as unprepared as I had been before. Except that this time it was not quite the same: like some primitive divine who suspects that the whole may not just be the sum of its individual parts, he went one step beyond his single performance and, that night after dinner, suddenly appeared before us in his full regalia, standing there not so much self-conscious as tense, not fully satisfied until we had nodded our approval at the total effect.

I told my parents then about the other occasions and my father said he had probably collected the whole outfit to impress his pals. It was not much of a conjecture because Simon did not seem to have any pals — and it was proved wrong on the following Sunday anyway, when he dressed, as usual, in the khaki working clothes we had bought him.

So, puzzled, we went on waiting — not too long this time, even a four or five hundred mile bus journey not as expensive as a black suit — until that day when my father paid him and he asked if he could send for his wife and child. We had never thought of him as married and his admission was like a sudden insight for us into the loneliness of that small two-roomed house at the bottom of our garden. The next day he sent off the money and six days later, little more than ten months after he himself had come to us, he brought them into the house to be introduced and to receive the always hoped-for present of tea and sugar and mealie meal.

The woman especially, tall and square boned, her skin quite black, like damp coal in the muggy evening light, did not fit into the small gentle picture that Simon had created of himself. She was dressed in probably the only new dress she owned — fresh from the old Singer sewing machine in the inevitable Indian trading store — their small son, too young to have clothes really his own and almost invisible behind the flimsy material of her skirt, draped in a cast-off man's singlet that was grey with age, the neck and arm holes partly sewn up to prevent it slipping right off his tiny body. Altogether, it was not exactly the family circle we had imagined; but in Simon's eyes at least it must have appeared more than satisfactory, and the first long phase of an episode we did not know existed was finally complete.

The missionary, therefore, had arrived at the lake's side complete with his wife and family, and Simon too was now ready to begin his own ministry. He began it, believe it or not, that very night. Our house bordered Shilanke township, a large African suburb, and as soon as he had washed up the dinner dishes and cleared away, he donned the only uniform it had been possible for him to choose and own and set off on the first of hundreds of journeys into that hectic and insanitary conglomeration of narrow dirt lanes and crumbling sun-baked mud houses.

It was rather like the way he had abruptly begun to work for us. True, it was the wife who completed his journey this time, but the result was about the same. Suddenly, from that night on, he became a kind of perfect apostle, answering so exactly to every letter of the law — right down to the bit where you promise to be fruitful and multiply — that in no time at all his wife was pregnant and growing larger by the day. Nor was that the least of his achievements, that passionate act — of love, as we were to see, not lust — figuring as it did somewhere outside a normal waking life that began at six in the morning and sped on until a little before midnight. Because none of those hours was spent idly, as I realized on the one afternoon I went with him into Shilanke, following as he hurried from house to house, knocking at the dirty board doorways until somebody came from the dim interior to listen, and then talking quickly and pointing to the open face of the Bible and explaining and talking some more until he was asked in or the door was closed in his face. I left him after only one hour, but there were three hours of it every afternoon and another three every evening, his rapid footsteps treading out a longer journey than ever.

Of course he could never have kept that pace up indefinitely. As it happened he was forced to slacken it after only nine months.

There is a false belief prevalent amongst Europeans in Africa that all African women give birth with swiftness and ease. This is probably why we did not worry when Simon's wife grew so hugely pregnant that she could do little more than sit in the shade of the guava tree while the first child played in the garden; perhaps it is even partly the reason why we did not notice that she had disappeared on that particular morning. It was more difficult to explain how we managed to overlook her absence during the remainder of the day. But somehow we did, and the first we knew of what was happening was when we were woken in the night by her scream. It was a long piercing scream, so drawn out that I enveloped it in a flash of fearful dream, woke with fright at my own vision, and still heard the end of it. I jumped up and ran down the passage to my parents' room. My father was lying in bed under a heap of blankets, recovering from an attack of malaria, but my mother was already up and putting on her dressing-gown.

"Go with your mother," my father said, "and find out what's going on. But be careful."

Still in my pyjamas, I led the way across the back garden. Before we reached the *kaia* the scream came again, short and sharp now, and my mother stopped me at the doorway and pushed me back against the side wall so I could not see inside. While I stood there in the darkness, listening, she went in alone. There was a furtive whisper of voices which stopped as soon as she entered. I heard her strike a match, and another, and a yellow glow shone out past me as the lamp flared. Then there was just her voice.

"Simon! Oh, Simon!"

No possible reply, just the cold unanswerable shock of it, quiet yet as protracted as the scream, followed by a silence of heavy strained breathing.

It was overcast and I could see nothing except the blob of light beside me and the dark outline of the house. I waited uneasily for several minutes and finally heard someone move inside. There was a rattle of wire or thin metal on concrete and a second later she came out again, holding something, not looking at me as she passed. I followed her, walking quickly to keep up; but she did not speak until she was back in the bedroom and by then, even by the light of the bedside lamp, I could see in her face what I had heard in her voice.

"She's in labour," she said. "She's been in labour since last night. And he didn't call us." She paused and said it again, as though we had not understood: "He didn't call us."

My father must have heard it as well then because he sat up in bed in spite of his fever. But she still did not explain immediately, just held out to him what she had brought in and let it drop beside the bed before he could reach out to touch or take it. It was a rough circle of light fencing wire, four or five strands thick, with chips of wood twisted into it at regular intervals, like screws that would wind the circle tighter when they were turned.

"They had that around her," she said, "around her stomach. They were tightening it and drawing it down to force the birth."

"They?" my father said.

But she did not want to say, because living in a comfortable house in a town you like to forget or ignore how slowly the irrational magic of superstition dies.

"Not even decent ones," she said. "Not even ones that at least regard themselves as doctors: two revolting old men who deal in filth and ignorance and fear."

She came over to where I was standing by the door.

"Call the police," my father said.

"No," she said, "that wouldn't do any good now."

"But why protect him?" he said. "When all that Bible stuff must have been for show, when it couldn't have meant anything?"

"No," she said. "It must have meant something because he waited a whole night and day before he called them. But what about from now on, what is it going to mean to him, how can he preach the Bible again after this?"

She never said that to him: only the once, to us, and my father lay down again, quietly, while she went back to the *kaia* and I went out to the kitchen to put water on to boil. I remember standing there by the stove in the middle of the night, dozing fitfully because it was no good searching for a reasonable explanation, no simple or obvious relation between the preacher, the perfect workman, and the husband of the woman who had screamed out and woken us earlier — no more than there had been between the man who had walked, penniless, four or five hundred miles and afterwards stood helpless in that very kitchen. So when the water boiled, I took the pots out and left them on the *kaia* step — still forbidden to enter — and afterwards slept in the cane chair in the corner of my parents' bedroom.

My mother woke us again at four o'clock. She sounded tired.

"It's another son," she said. "I think they should be all right."

That was to both of us, my father still stirring awake. To me she said: "The old men are still there. I didn't have the energy to turf them out. But they should go easily now, with nothing left to stay for. Take a stick with you, just in case."

So while she undressed and got into bed, I rummaged around in the hall cupboard, making a lot of noise, as though I were looking for something heavy. But it was time, not defence, that I needed and when I went out into the garden again I was still empty-handed: not frightened as an African bred in the bush and in the villages of closely ringed huts would have been frightened; merely a sixteen-year-old boy, alone with the old half-believed stories flaring out in the darkness, unnerved enough to realize that a stick could not help me.

And despite my last-minute hopes they were still there in the badly lit *kaia*, as she had said: it was a bare room and I saw the hump of the occupied bed first, and Simon sitting on the stone floor beside it, and them last of all, in the far corner of the room.

"Get out," I said aloud, and they rustled like shadows in their corner without really moving or rising; and I said it again, louder, "Get out!" and they stood up, hesitated, and shambled into the middle of the room. But they were looking at Simon — who had not once raised his head — not at me. I remember the strong unpleasant smell of them — a smell of sweat and dust and the rank sap of burning wood — only two paces away, unaccountably revolting, the three of us so close together that we almost made a waiting group, I too waiting, momentarily and unreasonably expecting him to look up. When he didn't I said it once more, shouting it this time, "Get out!" and they shuffled over to the door and disappeared. But I could still imagine them outside, lurking again in the shadows, and now it seemed partly Simon's fault.

"How can you preach your damn Bible after this?" I shouted.

He looked up then and I realized straight away why my mother had said it to us and not to him: because he knew it already, a million times better than I ever would — something she must have recognized even before she loosened the wire that he, with grieved and divided affection, had stood back and watched being strangled on to the body of his wife; and because it was not for me to say anyway, not merely a hurtful and wasteful use of those frightened seconds, but a usurping of the one right he still had left after what he had done — which is why it was no good my trying to talk to him later, at that second and last and more important time.

As it was, he still exercised that right the next morning, though more or less unconsciously. It was the first time he had ever failed to call us, yet when we stumbled out to the kitchen, tired and disgruntled from lack of sleep, he was already there, crouched against the wall by the stove. It was my mother he was waiting for: as soon as she saw her he said it, *"Dona! Oh, Dona!"* matching her almost perfectly, sound for sound, yet with the meaning somehow the complement of everything she could have intended.

I half-expected him to get up after that, but he remained crouching there, like a child and an animal and a man together, crouched as only an African bred in the bush and unused to the luxury of chairs can crouch, right down on his heels, his knees above the level of his shoulders, unmoving, so totally unselfconscious that any humiliation I may feel at the recollection must of necessity come solely from my own mind. His face cradled in his hands, he peered between his fingers at the dull painted surface of the wall, refusing to look at us or at the light of the window. And yet it was not a proverbial turning to the wall, primitive and hopeless, but rather a kind of patient grief; it was as if he were waiting for time and the slow silence of his own unbearable thoughts to relent and show him, reflected in the opaque lustreless surface of the wall, the recreated image of the man he once had been.

During the whole of that time my mother looked after him. She began on that first morning by taking his Bible from where it had been left, almost symbolically, at the far end of the kitchen, and placing it at his feet; which was where she also placed his food and drink, regularly three times a day, not once hurrying him, until of his own choice he stood up at the end of the third day and quietly began again on his old household tasks.

But that was not all she did for him during that time: she also cared for the mother and the baby and the first child — the first child especially, in its initial horror of being outcast. I mention this really to show how impossible it is to number the different times she interceded for him. All that is certain is that by then she must have appeared to him as somebody special, unique, even somebody mysteriously chosen and set apart — the more so because she was European and I can't help reflecting on the dubious history of my own race in Central Africa. So that from then on he had a task over and above the saving of the heterogeneous souls of Shilanke township, a task all the more difficult because no matter how we may hold up our hands in horror at the thought of it, the fact remains that it would have been impossible for him, an uneducated African, without the bloated and flimsy confidence that town life gives to white and coloured alike, impossible I say for him even to conceive of approaching a European with a challenge of faith, even one he loved in purity and with the gratitude of redemption, regardless of how that European might have appeared to be teetering on the brink of an eternity the strangled cries of whose lost inhabitants doubtless rang in the ears of his mind.

He had to find another way then, with only one other

way left open to him. Yet it sounds inadequate if I state it simply, that he was the perfect servant; because what he did went beyond the mere meaning of the buying and cooking and serving and cleaning and washing and ironing — and later gardening, attempted and mastered in a blaze of summer flowers — which, to a lesser degree, were what we paid him for; misleading as well because if he really was serving two masters now — the anonymous American and his message undoubtedly one — then certainly that house was not the other; only what it had come to represent since the one blind night of error, a single white woman — the genesis of those well-fingered pages no gateway here — unapproachable except through the unresponsive bricks and mortar that surrounded her waking and asleep.

Let me put it another way therefore: it was a kind of domestic perfection that he aimed at — and possibly achieved — reflected undramatically in the grand yet quiet orderliness of our home, and in the smaller things as well, in an insignificant detail like the daily sweeping of the drive, accomplished not, as you might imagine, with an efficient number of swift strokes, but with a bewildering profusion of curved and garlanded ones that left the loose dust surface twirled and plaited into a binding woven net of ropen sand.

And shortly after that it was only those small details that I had any chance of noticing at all, because as soon as I turned sixteen I left home and moved three hundred miles north to work on the mines near the Congo border. I still went home, but only for short visits now, mainly at Christmas time when for a week or ten days I would fit easily back into my old place. In the mornings I would wake up and find the cup of tea he had already left beside my bed, and in the afternoons hear him walk past the house, down toward the township in that same black suit, and return again, punctually, in time to prepare the evening meal. It was all exactly the way I had left it: nothing about him seemed to change.

But there was some change during that time, in us, not in him: in my mother especially, who suddenly developed a heart complaint and was warned by the doctor to rest and avoid all excitement. When she wrote and told me about it I don't think I gave Simon a thought, too worried about her and my father and myself as well, about the closed family group that wasn't closed anyway, not any more. So that I should have remembered him, at least after the first shock I should have, if only out of regard for her. But I didn't, not then nor later, in that October towards the end of my fourth year at work.

It was a hot summer, one of the worst Octobers I could remember — they said afterwards that that, the heat, had a lot to do with what happened. I only learned about it in the late afternoon when I arrived home from work and found the African messenger waiting outside the door of my single quarters with the telegram. It was a short message, to the point: it said my mother had had a heart attack while resting and had died in her sleep. Looking back now, I seem to have read the telegram and climbed back into my car and driven the three hundred miles to Lusaka all in one unbroken action, because the next thing I remember clearly is arriving at the house late at night. It was in darkness and I let myself in at the front door and walked hesitantly along the front verandah to my parents' bedroom; from there I wandered slowly through the lingering familiarity of the other rooms. To begin with I thought I was alone, but when I reached the kitchen I was immediately conscious of somebody there before me. I knew instantly it was Simon, without needing to look; but I turned on the light just the same and it was exactly as it had been before, with him crouched down against the wall beside the stove, his face turned from both me and the light. Even the Bible was in the same place, on the table at the far end of the kitchen.

"Get up Simon," I said, and when he didn't answer I took the book and placed it at his feet as my mother had done. But he kicked it away, not daring to touch it with his hands. I remembered that other night then and what I had said, and I took it back to the table and afterwards put some food and drink in its place. But when he pushed those aside also, I left him there in the darkness and went in search of my father.

I found him at the home of a friend and stayed with him there until the day of the funeral. He said that the thought of the house frightened him now, but on the way back from the funeral he suddenly changed his mind and we turned out of the long line of cars and made our own way slowly home. Already, in the daylight, it was looking different, deserted and with the driveway unswept for the first time in years. That more than anything else gave me the feeling that he was still there, and I took my father in at the front door, deciding on the spur of the moment to keep him away from the kitchen for as long as possible. It was not difficult: he was too upset to go walking about the house; and I left him resting in the lounge while I went to the kitchen on the pretext of making tea.

I was right: he was still there, crouched in exactly the same place, not even looking round when I entered. The only change was the tin cup half full of water on the floor beside him, which his wife must have left for him. I put some bread beside it and this time he did not push it away. The Bible was there too, unmoved, on the table.

"She's gone Simon," I said.

But again he did not answer, dry-eyed and silent.

My father on the other hand talked and cried most of

the afternoon, constantly harking back, his crying a little like the way he shouted when he was excited, loud and sharp and sudden, yet prolonged once it had begun. I hoped I would have some relief from it that night, but he refused to go into his own bedroom and I ended up making him a bed on the other side of my own room. We lay there only yards apart and every time I was beginning to doze off he would jerk up in bed and break out, "I can't believe it, that she's really gone, that she won't walk through that door and say it was all a joke."

It was what he had already said a hundred times that day, yet what there had been no need to say — what it had been most necessary not to say — even once; each repetition like a perverse self-torment, unforgetting and infectious, like Simon's hopeless and lonely still-wakeful vigil — because at that time I had no good reason for suspecting that Simon's distress was in any way different, anything other than the same unbearably simple grief; both of them, apparently, the one with his tears and the other with his silence, united in a determination not to relinquish her.

And yet even then, there in the middle of the night, I might possibly have seen my mistake without needing to be told, if only I had remembered the Bible, considered just for a moment what it had signified on that other occasion. But somehow I overlooked it, and it was not until the next afternoon, when my father unexpectedly followed me into the kitchen, that I discovered the real nature and extent of my own error.

I think the first sight of Simon crouched there like that shocked my father more than it had me.

"How long has he been here?" he asked quickly.

"Since the day she died," I said.

"But he can't stay here like this," he said, genuinely concerned.

He went over and tried to pull Simon to his feet, but his body was limp and impossible to move.

"He'll move when he's ready," I said. "I don't think we can hurry him."

"But we can't just leave him here like this in the meantime," he said, his voice already beginning to rise.

He looked quickly round the kitchen, saw the Bible, and brought it back to Simon.

"Here," he said, holding it out, "take it back to your *kaia*."

But at the sight of it Simon had turned his face resolutely toward the dark wall.

"Why doesn't he want it?" he said.

He had never been a religious man and now he riffled uncertainly through the worn pages, vaguely searching, discovering nothing.

"Here," he said again, "take it. That's what the *Dona* would want, the way she did before."

He held the Bible out further, so that it actually touched the limp khaki shirt. Simon shuddered away from it.

"No, *Bwana*," he said, and it was as if he had had to force the words out against his will. He began to cry softly straight afterwards.

"Leave him," I said.

"How can we?" my father said. "He's been here too long already. How can we leave him?"

So he tried once more, proffered him the book a third time: and this time he did not pull away, nor accept it either, the unnerving tears falling between his knees on to the blood red polish of the stone floor.

"Take it," my father said, and I actually saw him waver and give in.

"Not Heaven, *Bwana*," he said brokenly, "not Heaven."

And suddenly it was unmistakable, his reason for crouching there for three days and three nights.

"Heaven?" my father said, puzzled.

"No, *Bwana*," he said, "not Heaven."

"Don't give him the Bible," I said quickly.

But it was too late because he had already snatched it, scooped it up and pressed it, crumpled it desperately against his thin chest. My father did not try to stop him.

"He means Hell," he said incredulously; and then to Simon himself: "You mean Hell?"

Yet even after three days of lonely struggle, the black book finally clutched in both hands, he still could not bring himself to say it properly, fully.

"Not Heaven, *Bwana*," he repeated almost mechanically, "not Heaven."

But that was enough, and just for a moment I thought that my father was going to hit him. Instead, without a word, he did what he had threatened to do almost six years before: grabbed him and dragged him across the kitchen and threw him outside. I had a brief glimpse of him staggering across the driveway, close to that spot where I had first seen him, and then the door was slammed closed and my father was leaning against it, as though physically excluding whatever it was Simon had abruptly come to stand for in his eyes.

"How could he say that?" he said hollowly. "About her of all people?"

"He had to," I said.

"Had to!" he shouted. "After everything she did for him!"

"It was a choice then," I said, "between her and that black book. Between her and his faith."

"Faith! What faith! The one she gave back to him after he'd thrown it away?"

"Yes, that one: because it was still partly his. If he'd admitted her, one of the unchosen, the unredeemed —

I don't know what he calls them — then he would have had to discard it all, the work, the preaching, the whole faith. There would have been so little left."

"And even that would have come from her. Who saved his wife and gave him his son if it wasn't her?"

"All right," I said. "There would have been nothing left, nothing of his own."

"And now?" he said. "Do you really think he has anything left now, after what he's done to her?"

"Done to her?" I said. "But that's believing what he believes! Isn't it what he's done to himself that matters now?"

"No," he said, "because we're worried about her now, not him."

Which was so true and so false that it was pointless to go on arguing — because in a way it was the choice re-enacted, not pondered over or wrestled with for three days, but decided in a split second and with Simon the rejected one this time.

"So you're throwing him out for good?" I said.

"Yes, for good. I don't want him back in this house again. Not after what he said. I want you to go up there for me today and tell him to leave."

But fortunately that was one job I never had to carry out, because barely an hour later Simon's wife walked past the lounge windows and stopped out on the front drive. She had a bundle of belongings balanced on her head and the two children with her, the younger one carried on her back in the traditional sling. We both knew what that meant and when, a few minutes later, we heard the back door open and close my father said, "You go out. I don't want to see him. Pay him off as best you can."

I found him waiting in the dark passage between the kitchen and the dining-room, dressed in his black suit and with the leather case and broad-brimmed hat gripped tightly in both hands.

"I'm sorry, *Bwana*," he said.

He was still crying softly, his black-brown face puffy and swollen.

"It's all right, Simon," I said, because really there was nothing I could say.

I took out my wallet and gave him what money I had — I don't know how much — and he put it into his pocket without even looking at it.

"I'm sorry, *Bwana*," he said again. "I'm sorry, *Bwana*."

I left him then, letting him leave the house in his own time and fashion, and went through to the front verandah. My father, hearing me go past the lounge, called out bitterly:

"Did you ask him if he can still preach religion after what he's done?"

It was not unlike what I had said four years earlier — though meant only for my ears in this case. But I think the sound must have carried through the house because a few seconds later the kitchen door opened and closed rapidly and Simon hurried out to where his wife was waiting.

I had expected to see some other belongings, but apart from the clothes they wore that one bundle was all that they owned and they left in the way they had come, on foot. I watched them, the four of them, Simon out in front, walk slowly down the unswept drive, cross the tar road that led to town, and disappear into Shilanke. Which was at least an appropriate kind of exit, that place and its people a part of the idea for which he had rejected his own instinctive love and gratitude. But whether he stayed there and for how long I couldn't say, because I never saw him again, never even heard anything about him, he and his family and his few paltry possessions stepping back into that unknown hinterland just as abruptly as they had emerged from it.

True, I often wonder about him, try to work out what he must be doing or where he is, but most of that is pure conjecture. The only thing I know with any degree of certainty, the one thing I can't bring myself to doubt, is that he has never gone back to Nyasaland, never returned to that village on the shores of the lake. How could he, after what he had set out to do? — because it is one thing to forget the dead (to banish them to death as it were) in order to go on living; and quite another thing to consign them to Hell. What could he say to that missionary who had sent him out? That he had traded one eternity of lost life for a hundred or a thousand other lives, exchanged the one for the ninety-nine? Or worse still, that when it came to the point he wasn't really able to help the other ninety-nine either, having cast out the one that mattered? I don't know. I find it hard to put myself in his place. Sometimes I imagine him trying to atone with pure quantity, adding name after rescued name to an interminable heart-breaking list — but a meaningless list just the same, never the simple passport he wants to make it.

Because he never will go back, nor arrive anywhere either. And that journey which started out as a journey to somewhere and something is now just a journey, nothing more, endless; with the dust kicked up by his heels — the same dust that I once imagined massed into low hills — risen by now into towering craggy peaks, impassable; so that somehow, whenever I think of him, no matter how I try to picture him, he always seems to be walking.

# The Jackal Fence

He arrived back at the house late at night. He hadn't been there since the morning of the accident and in the car lights it looked gloomy and deserted. As he opened the door leading onto the front verandah he felt a little sorry for himself, and also slightly drunk after an evening at the Club. "I have to go back sometime," he'd said earlier, over a glass of whiskey. They had tried to dissuade him. "Listen Watson, put it off for a while," Jenkins had said. "Give yourself a chance to get over the funeral and the inquiry." But he'd insisted — it was time he started living with the truth; the sooner the better. He'd been conscious as he spoke of sounding rather brave. "Pluck," old Lloyd-Jones had called it, "the man's got pluck." He had felt flattered, even though the old man had added a few minutes later: "The young'uns died like flies in India, of course; worse than here if you didn't get them into the hills." Still, he'd been very decent at the inquiry. Jenkins too. "It's just a formality," he'd said. "We'll get you through it in a few minutes." And old Lloyd-Jones: "Give me only the facts, as simply as you can." He'd been grateful for that. "I was reversing the car," he'd told them, "early in the morning. I looked, but the rear-view mirror was clear. I felt this bump on the back wheels and then on the front. And he was there on the drive. The girl, the nanny, ran over and picked him up, but he was dead." "And you're quite sure the rear-view mirror was clear?" Lloyd-Jones had asked. Yes, he was sure. There was more: the girl had had blood on her hands, and she'd screamed at him in Bemba, something he didn't understand. He hadn't wanted to touch the child; he'd let her carry it into the house. But he didn't tell them any of that. Nor about Kitty, how she hadn't just gone to England on holiday.

"The bitch!" he said aloud, standing alone on the dark verandah.

Death through misadventure, they'd decided. Jenkins had told him beforehand: "There's no question of blame in this kind of situation." But he went on feeling uneasy about it just the same — a child couldn't simply die; and he hadn't dared to touch him afterwards. Now he wandered unhappily through the unlit house. She had no right to clear out, he thought resentfully, leaving him on his own with a child and only a young girl to look after it. Letting that happen to him. He came to Michael's bedroom: the door was open and he closed it hastily and went quickly through to the kitchen at the other end of the house. The outside door was also open. That surprised him. He was sure he'd locked up thoroughly before he left. He switched on the outside light and heard someone jump off the back step. He peered out nervously: she was standing at the edge of the shadows, on the hard red earth, facing him.

"What the hell are you still doing here!" he shouted at her.

She was a young African girl, no more than seventeen, dressed in a cheap cotton dress. She had nothing on underneath it — he noticed that even then — and her feet were bare. Her small round head, the hair close-cropped, looked peculiarly childish and immature.

"Didn't I tell you to get out of here?" he said.

She didn't answer and it occurred to him that she hadn't said a word since the accident. He fumbled in his wallet, took out several notes, and threw them on the step.

"That's all I owe you," he said. "Take it and go. I wish I'd never seen you."

The girl made no move to pick up the money.

"Bloody cheek," he said. "Expecting to be paid. After what . . . after what you . . ."

He suddenly began to cry and he turned away and went through to his own bedroom. He felt lonely and hard done by. He switched on the light and noticed for the first time how bare the room was. No pictures on the walls; nothing personal about it. Like a cell. He thought how Kitty would have arranged it and made it more comfortable — looked after everything, Michael as well. The resentment and the brooding unease flared up together. She shouldn't have gone, he thought. She should have been there . . . here, with me. Who else was to blame? That ignorant girl outside? What did she know or care? And he, himself? For a moment he wasn't sure, and then it came to him, with unexpected clarity: if Kitty hadn't gone, Michael would still be alive. It was so simple that he wondered why he hadn't seen it before. The simple logic of it. With sudden resolution he sat down at the small desk under the window and began the letter he'd been putting off for several days.

"Dear Kitty," he wrote, "You will have received my telegrams, so this isn't a letter of explanation." He paused, intent on choosing the right words. Only inches from his bowed head, at the open window, small brown beetles and moths crawled ineffectually across the fine gauze screen. "Now that it's all over, I feel morally compelled to tell you that I hold you fully responsible for the death of our son. Had you not deserted him, left him to some incompetent African girl, he would almost certainly be alive today." He considered saying something more about the girl outside (why on earth didn't she go?), but scrapped the idea. "There is, of course, nothing to be gained from lengthy recriminations. Nonetheless, I do feel that you have, by your actions, severed the last bond between us. I therefore leave it to your conscience to decide whether or not you owe me a divorce. For my part, I can see nothing to prevent it."

He read it through and was pleased. It had the right sound — decisive, direct, conveying exactly that sense of surety he'd been groping after for days. He addressed it and sealed the envelope and propped it up on the dressing table. It gave him a sense of relief, just looking at it. He forgot about the African girl outside. Lying in bed in the darkness, he thought nostalgically of Michael — of how he'd loved him; of all the things he would have done for him.

The feeling of relief survived the night. The next day, sitting in his office at the Public Works Department, he calculated ten days for the letter to reach England and at least another ten days before he received a reply. In some inexplicable way it was a kind of reprieve. He didn't quite understand why — only that he felt less uneasy, more free. As though he had successfully disposed of an unwanted burden. He even felt capable, for the first time, of visiting Michael's grave. He had shrunk from the idea before — much as he had shrunk from touching the small body when the girl held it.

He went that very afternoon. The cemetery was a cleared space in the bush, surrounded by a ten foot high jackal fence. The sight of the fence shocked him a little. He sensed what it was for and quickly dismissed the image it conjured. He felt better once he was inside, walking along the clean concrete path towards the small group of neatly ordered gravestones. The marble tablet was a mottled white, in the stylized shape of a Roman scroll. He liked it, its rather faded, old-world appearance; it might almost have been there for years. Slowly he read the inscription: "A Beloved Son, Michael

Watson. Aged Two Years." A warm tide of emotion seemed to rise in his throat and he had to force back the tears. It was not an unpleasant sensation.

The warm sense of loss remained with him throughout the following weeks. Outside of working hours he spent most of his time at the Club. They were very good to him there. They didn't ask him about Kitty and carefully avoided mentioning Michael. "No better place for you," old Lloyd-Jones said. "The important thing at a time like this is to stay cheerful." He did his best, going to the house only to sleep. The girl still hadn't gone. He heard her moving about at the back of the house, and once, as he was going to his bedroom, he came face to face with her in the passage.

"What do you want from me?" he asked.

She wouldn't answer, wouldn't even look at him. She was wearing the same dress and he could smell the strong unwashed scent of her skin. As she sidled past him he grasped her arm. But she pulled away and ran through to the kitchen. The encounter disturbed him, and his mind, almost automatically now, reverted to Kitty. She has a lot to answer for, he thought, walking out on me like that. Sometimes, at night, just as he was falling asleep, he was woken by small, furtive sounds outside the door. But he usually forgot them by morning.

He mentioned the problem of the girl at the Club. "Don't waste your time trying to understand them," old Lloyd-Jones said. "It was the same in India. They have their own ways of doing everything. They're not like us." Jenkins was slightly more practical. "Just forget to pay her at the end of the month," he said. "She'll soon go. And in the meantime you have a housekeeper." That was true: in the few waking hours he did spend at home, he'd noticed that she continued to keep the house clean and tidy. "Legally, of course," Jenkins added, "you can make her get out." "Yes," he said vaguely, "I suppose I could." But he was unwilling, for some reason, to confront her.

Then, exactly three weeks after he had written, he received Kitty's reply. He waited until lunchtime, when the office was empty, before he read it. It was much longer and more personal than his own letter and it upset him terribly. That night he drank more than usual at the Club and didn't get home until nearly one o'clock.

It was a warm humid night and the flying ants had crawled in under the verandah door. When he turned on the light in the lounge, they whirled aimlessly round and round the globe. He slumped down in the Morris chair and watched them spiralling down as they lost their wings. The letter was still in his pocket. He took it out and looked at it again. "I can't possibly express," she began, "how hurt I was by your letter. I wouldn't have believed that you could be so cruel and unjust." He turned over to the next page: "I didn't desert Michael. You'll admit that if you're honest. I told you while we were still on leave, I couldn't stand another three years on a bush station. You knew that and yet you still made us go back." He looked further on: "Why am I more to blame than you? It was you who kept Michael there. I wanted to bring him back with me. I can't help thinking sometimes that you used him."

He threw the letter down on the red-polished cement floor. Why did she have to write to him at all? Why couldn't she just have given him a divorce? He felt unhappy and confused. He remembered the small, almost quaint gravestone — surrounded by the high jackal fence and the threatening line of bush. Outside, in the darkness, thousands of insects screamed at him incessantly.

"This bloody country," he said desperately. "It destroys everything in the end."

He felt something touching his bare skin and he pulled up his trouser leg. One of the ants that had lost its wings was crawling up through the hairs on the back of his calf. He knocked it off and crushed it under his foot. The touch of it, the soft yellow-brown body, horrified him.

At that moment he heard a noise somewhere in the back of the house. He walked quickly through to the kitchen. She was crouched down in the far corner, under the window, looking sleepy and miserable. As he came in and turned on the light, she stood up.

"You and your bloody country!" he said menacingly.

She tried to dart past him, but he caught her by the wrist. He could smell the familiar unwashed scent of her body.

"You killed him between you, didn't you!" he said.

She tried to pull away, the soft pink palm of her open hand turned towards him as she strained to break free. He remembered the blood on her fingers and with his free hand he hit her across the side of the head. She let out a strange frightened sound and drew back against the wall.

"If it wasn't for you he'd be alive!" he shouted, and hit her again, harder.

She half fell, clutching at his leg to save herself; but he shook her off, and as she lay at his feet he kicked her. She screamed loudly, like a child in pain, and he kicked her twice more. The third time, she merely grunted and lay still.

He was leaning against the cool plaster wall, breathing heavily. He felt dizzy, but also relieved. Just for a minute or two he experienced the same sense of reprieve that had followed the writing of the letter. "What does she know or care?" he murmured to himself. "She probably doesn't even remember." But this time the feeling didn't last. Very gradually, he became aware of the silence in the room. He opened his eyes. She was lying directly below him, her side touching the wall. Bending down, he shook her roughly, but she didn't move or speak. Something seemed to coil slowly out from under her dress, near the top of her thighs, snaking along a slight depression in the floor towards him. It was warm and wet to touch. He looked at his fingers and found they were coated with blood.

He rushed over to the tap and washed his hand clean. Already the blood had formed into a small round pool. For a short time he stood there helplessly watching her, then finally he went and rang the doctor. Afterwards he couldn't bring himself to go back into the kitchen. Instead, he poured himself a drink and walked up and down the front verandah trying to invent a plausible explanation. He felt like a schoolboy again, having to explain some absurd misdemeanour — he refused to consider what would happen if she died. But when the doctor arrived he had failed to think up anything convincing.

"She had a fall," he mumbled lamely as he took him through to the kitchen.

He waited apprehensively in the lounge for half an hour. When the doctor came out, he jumped nervously to his feet.

"Is she all right?" he asked.

"She's as well as can be expected after a miscarriage," he said.

"A miscarriage?"

He didn't understand for a moment.

"Yes, didn't you know she was carrying a child?" The doctor looked at him doubtfully.

"But she couldn't . . . " he began, then collected himself. "I had no idea," he added.

They carried her to the outside room between them. It looked unexpectedly deserted, as though nobody had lived in it for some weeks. There was dust over everything and no linen, not even a blanket, on the torn mattress.

"The way these people live!" the doctor said.

He fetched fresh bed linen from the house and together they made her as comfortable as possible.

"You've been awfully kind," Watson said before he left.

The doctor looked at him curiously.

"You realize, of course," he said, "that I'll have to report this?"

"Oh yes, I fully understand."

But it was what he'd been dreading.

Jenkins came round the next morning, early, before he left for the office.

"I spoke to the doctor last night," he said.

"Yes, I know."

"Don't look so worried," he said, and laughed. "This isn't an inquisition. Just tell me what happened, that's all. The basic facts. I can't do anything for you until I know."

Suddenly he liked Jenkins more than ever — he should have remembered how dependable he was before the inquiry.

"You know how cut up I've been about Michael," he began. "Well it's stayed in my mind all along that she was to blame. After all, she was his nanny; she was supposed to be watching him. I've tried to forget, but having her around here all the time, I couldn't. Anyway, last night everything seemed to come to a head. I'd had a bit too much to drink and when I saw her in the kitchen I just set about her."

"You didn't know she was expecting a child?"

"I had no idea."

"Look here, old man," Jenkins said — he put his hand affectionately on Watson's shoulder. "Personally, I understand the situation. But there is a legal angle. If she decides to lay a complaint, I have to do something about it. So my advice to you — unofficially mind — is to pay her off. Give her enough money to keep her quiet and get rid of her."

"Yes," he said, "I suppose that would be best."

After Jenkins had gone, he sat quietly in the Morris chair, thinking for some time. It had gone off better than he'd hoped. What a fool he'd been to lie awake half the night worrying. At one point, he'd even considered telling Jenkins everything — about the child as well. It would just have complicated everything needlessly. In any case, how could anybody be sure about a thing like that. He remembered what old Lloyd-Jones had said: "Promiscuity isn't the word. There's not one mother's son of them knows who his father is." And it had only happened the once — soon after Kitty left. He'd been drunk then too, and lonely. God, how lonely he'd been, with the responsibility of the child on his hands. He hadn't even meant to go that far; all he'd wanted was some human contact. She shouldn't have made such a fuss, fighting and kicking like that. He couldn't help losing control. What did she expect? And then, afterwards, drooping around the house as though the end of the world had come, as though he'd injured her for life. Listless for weeks, showing no interest in anything. Not even Michael . . .

For a second or two the same half-formulated fear that had plagued him during the night flashed back into his mind. He gripped the arms of the chair and leaned forward.

But Jenkins had said that virginity didn't mean anything to these people. He should know — all the years he'd spent here. So that wasn't an excuse. How could it be? There were no excuses for her. She should have been watching. He'd been right to get angry — many people would have acted sooner. Though once again he'd gone too far. He admitted that. And what did it achieve after all? Even if he'd tried to explain, she probably wouldn't have known what he was talking about. Like beating his head against the wall.

He glanced down and noticed the fine transparent wings, discarded by the ants, littering the floor. They reminded him of his train of thought on the previous evening. "This bloody country," he said aloud. But his voice conveyed nothing of his earlier desperation.

During the following days he gradually recaptured his former ease of mind. In one sense he was slightly happier, because he no longer felt quite so indignant with Kitty. On Jenkins' advice, he collected some money from the bank and put it into a plain brown envelope. He didn't give it to her straight away, however: he waited until she was on her feet and walking tentatively round the garden. "It's a present," he said. "Take it and go away. I don't need you here any more." She accepted it without a word, but she showed no signs of preparing to leave. She'll probably recuperate first, he thought. But at the end of a week she was still there.

For the first time he felt genuinely puzzled. What did she want? What kept her there? There didn't seem to be anything. Unless . . . An idea suddenly occurred to him: perhaps he was the reason. He dismissed it immediately, as absurd. But it kept recurring, and the more he thought about it the more likely it seemed. It even attracted him slightly, the idea of her waiting silently at the house, secretly watching him come and go. He remembered the furtive noises outside his door and the night he met her in the passage. Her listlessness too, before the accident — it would explain that — something beyond his control, a stroke of fate.

He began coming home a little earlier from the Club. One evening, instead of going in through the front door, he went round to the back. She was sitting on the outside step in the darkness, and before she realized he was there, he was crouching beside her.

"What are you waiting here for?" he asked quietly.

She remained silent. In the dim light he could just see that her face was turned away. He placed one hand gently on her bare leg and felt her stiffen.

"It's all right," he said reassuringly.

Tentatively, he eased the other hand round her shoulders, but she twisted away and tried to slide off the side of the steps. For a moment he held her, pressing her down onto the concrete, feeling her go passive underneath him.

"That's better," he said softly, and then felt a sharp pain in his neck, as she bit him. "You bitch!" he shouted, pulling back, letting her slip away from him, out of reach.

He thought she would run for the outside room and he jumped up and tried to block her path. Instead, she slipped through the open door into the house. He chased after her, but she was too quick, running into Michael's room and locking the door behind her. He stopped abruptly, hardly able to believe his eyes.

"Come out of there!" he shouted. "Get out of his room!"

He felt outraged. That she should dare to go into Michael's room. She, of all people. Who had less right than anybody, after what she'd done — who hadn't even shown she'd understood or cared, least of all been sorry.

"Come out!" he shouted again, punching at the door.

He waited, breathing heavily, but no sound reached him through the heavy wood panelling. Still angry, he ran round to the back of the house and tried to peer into the room from outside, but the curtains were drawn. Impatiently, he ripped off the gauze screen and forced open the window. As he did so, the lower pane broke and cut him across the back of the hand. In his haste and excitement, he barely noticed what had happened. With blood running from the wound, he dragged the curtain aside and climbed into the darkened room. He could just make out her slight form, standing by the door, frightened, clinging to the handle. But something else attracted his attention — in the shadows to his left, out of sight of anybody looking in from the passage — some kind of bed or pallet made up on the floor. He strode over and switched on the wall light. In the corner, close to the legs of the cot, was a narrow kapok mattress covered with a dingy grey blanket. At the head of the crudely made bed was a line of bricks on which were placed a few personal trifles — a coloured bead necklace, a gourd rattle, a creased, much-handled photograph of a child. The meaning of it all didn't sink in for a moment. He crouched down, close to the grey blanket, and became aware of the strong, distinctive smell of her body. It slowly occurred to him, then, what he had found — why she had stayed on in the house, why he had so often heard furtive noises in the passage at night. It was because she lived and slept there, in Michael's room. Here, close to the memory of his son, where the small body had lain after the accident. The idea appalled him — he didn't quite know why — like an act of desecration.

He rushed over to the door, opened it, and tried to push her out into the passage.

"You leave this room!" he shouted. "For good! I don't want you in here! Ever!"

She struggled, but he was too heavy for her. In the darkened passage, she suddenly fell onto her knees and took his hand, kissing it — the one he had cut, streaked now with blood.

"Please, *Bwana,*" she said, "please." And then something in Bemba he didn't understand — repeating it over and over, the same thing she'd said on the day of the accident.

But he pulled his hand away, refusing to listen, and locked the bedroom door. She was crying now.

"You have no right to go in there," he said, his voice choked with indignation. "No right!"

Ignoring her tears and pleading, he forced her down the passage and pushed her roughly into the lounge. She fell in the darkness, and before she could get up he closed and locked the intervening door.

Back in his own bedroom, he could still hear her crying. Occasionally she beat half-heartedly against the door. But he tried not to hear. He turned on the bright overhead light and lay down on the bed. In some indefinable way he felt betrayed. He thought bitterly: what did I expect, letting her stay here all the time? What does she know about losing a child? Lloyd-Jones was right — they took advantage of you. Well not any more. And to think that he'd blamed Kitty for what she'd done to them. Well it wasn't too late even now to change all that.

In his mind he began to compose another letter: "My dearest Kitty, Now that the initial pain of losing Michael has eased a little, I've come to see things differently. I realize that I shouldn't have written as I did." He paused. He had ceased altogether to hear the faint cries from the lounge. After all, he thought, it's only right that she should see his grave — it was the least he could do for her. He pictured to himself the simple gravestone with its old-world air and moving inscription: "A Beloved Son". Tears came into his eyes. It would be some consolation to her; he was sure of that.

The thought soothed him. Outside, the crying and pleading had finally stopped; and gradually, in the heavy silence, he dozed and fell asleep. He didn't hear her leave the house, her bare feet lightly brushing the back steps as she stole round to the open window. Quietly, she climbed into the room, taking care to avoid the jagged edge of broken glass, and lay down on the narrow mattress — curled up like a child beside the cot. It was where she had spent every night since the child's death — lying passively in the shadow of the smaller mattress just above her head. As always, the room was in darkness. Now, however, she did not sleep. Silent, breathing lightly, almost inaudibly, she lay awake, her child's eyes wide open, staring fearfully at the window, at the broken pane.

# A Nehru Shirt

"This is not your place," he said — with her dark shadow moving noiselessly to and fro behind him. But what place? That dull and orderly row of European-style houses built before Independence? Or the untidy, sprawling life of Shilembe township, audible even above our raised voices, separated from us only by a narrow strip of tarred road? Probably neither of us knew. We were too angry at the time, locked in a battle of wills which blurred any differences of race and origin — which kept her confined to those shadowy regions forever.

It was not always like that. When I first went there, on a neighbourly visit, he greeted me with instant and unfeigned friendliness, opening the door wide for me to enter even before I could give my name. I remember that he, Aaron, was dressed in a collarless, loose white shirt, Indian in style. He noticed me admiring it.

"My sister made it," he said, bringing her forward, out of the shadows, with a peremptory movement of his hand.

She was of medium height, with features which were somehow a mixture of African and Arab, finely formed, her nose almost oriental in the way it curved delicately above her full lips.

I made my first mistake then.

"A real mixing of the cultures," I said.

"Excuse me" — in a puzzled tone, his voice instantly formal, distant.

"I mean the shirt," I said, "your sister making a Nehru shirt."

He laughed pleasantly, as one might at a pathetically naive person.

"You are mistaken," he explained. "This is a traditional African shirt."

"I have always heard them described as Nehru shirts, after . . ."

He interrupted me, not rudely.

"Ah, you have a lot to learn, my friend."

That was one argument I never pursued with him. I was too busy watching his sister, Mina, hoping she would sit and talk with us. But he dismissed her with a sharp click of the tongue. As she faded back into the darkened portion of the house, he placed one arm warmly across my shoulders and led me to a chair. "A friend of Africa," he called me then, taking my silence for acquiescence.

Perhaps I might have been. In those early days of our acquaintance, we used to sit out on the screened verandah (the noise of Shilembe township, turbulent and colourful, drifting up towards us) and discuss the problems of African emergence.

"You wish always to impose your Western methods," he used to say. "What you have to learn is how to think Black."

He was marvellously black: a handsome bull of a man in his spotlessly white Nehru shirt; expressing himself not only through his speech, but with his eyes and with his large well-made hands — the delicate pink of his palms reflecting the soft flesh tones of his open mouth; his tongue red-pink between even rows of teeth.

"To think Black. That is the answer. The door through which you have to pass. To see it all as it truly is, all of this."

Waving his hand . . . at what? At the unimaginative rectangle of house in which we sat? Or the evening sky, purple-red, ornamented with strips of black cloud and with the topmost feathery tufts of gum trees? Or the dim rows of picturesque and insanitary huts beneath? I was never sure on that point. While all around us the uncertain evening light faded rapidly into night.

"It will be revealed to you then," he used to say, "when the door is opened."

At regular intervals throughout such evenings, his hand would beckon backwards into the near darkness, commandingly, to where Mina waited. I would detect the faint sweet smell of her body beside me; so close when she removed the glasses from the table. Never speaking. As silent as he had ever wished. The two of us sitting stolidly in our cane chairs (even he graceless beside my memory of her), waiting for her mute service to be done. Within moments she would be gone again, leaving us alone in the warm still night, facing the invisible township, the distant voices reaching us through the tuneless background screech of insect noise.

We were always formal at the end, when we could no longer see each other. "An image of African womanhood," he said of her once, admiringly. I was standing in the open doorway, about to depart. "A true daughter of the people."

Later, in my own neighbouring cottage, I could hear those same people in the township flanking the road. Sometimes the drumming lasted all night. Lying in my single bed, I would listen to the general commotion: to the women screaming drunken imprecations at their men or laughing at some hidden, secret pleasure.

"A condition of freedom," I called it then, to him. But only tentatively — peculiarly unsure of myself whenever I tried to defend that one small privilege — the simple right of ordinary people to squabble and joke and make love in the uncontrollable darkness.

"It is what we must protect them from," he countered, his large, heavy hand extended out over the vague silhouette of shanties and thatched huts. "Protection from their own inner chaos. From personal servitude. That is the true condition of their freedom."

Even then, opening the fundamental debate. But only in theory. Not letting it probe through to my own life and experience. Probably because I never thought of her as needing to be free. Partly that. It seemed an old dead debate where she was concerned.

I used to watch her in the garden in the early afternoon. I would sit by the gauze screen of the open window and simply look at her. She always wore the same style of clothing: a dress-cloth of brightly coloured African print, covering one shoulder and reaching down to her bare feet; and a length of the same material wrapped around her head in a loose turban.

I'm sure she knew I was there watching. As she did during my final meeting with Aaron: working in the kitchen at the back while we argued, as though unconcerned by the raised voices — even when he took hold of me and threw me against the side wall. Perhaps a slight stiffening of her back and neck when the low table broke and I called out her name. An involuntary cry, not really appealing to her.

She preserved exactly that calm equanimity in the garden. Placid. Essentially the same silent figure out there in the sunlight as in the house — I realize that now — identical to the obedient shadow who waited at table, who wordlessly brought and collected the glasses on the warm evenings. An image of African womanhood. Yet in those early days I never really merged my two visions of her into one. They seemed so alien: the humble servant, shy and retiring, unprotesting, a mere presence before his hearth; and the young woman who knelt lovingly in the garden, the soft pads of her bare heels coated with reddish powdery dust, her hands, as fine and black-pink as his, delicately fingering the soil, pressing down the earth around the roots of the young plants.

I would never have thought of speaking to her alone while he was at home; nor of disturbing her in that sunlit garden where she was always so solitary — the trees casting broken, restless shadows across the ground all about her. But his absence and the darkness emboldened me. That, and her suddenly appearing there at the very edge of the garden the first night he was away.

"You shouldn't be out here," I said.

"It is such a hot night," she answered quietly.

I took her reply as a flimsy excuse, though it was in fact warm and breathless, the still scent of hibiscus and dust strong in the air.

"You should be more careful so close to the township," I said — that, too, was a night of drums. "The men will soon be coming along the road from the bars."

"They are my people," she said.

Acquiescent in that as in all things. The same when I reached out and touched her breast, sliding my hand beneath the thin cloth on to her warm flesh. She didn't protest or draw back.

"Be still," I said, "I won't hurt you."

And she remained unmoving: so calm and quiet that I interpreted her readiness as desire — as perhaps it might have been — pulling her gently towards me; placing her smooth bare arms around my neck; her broad shapely lips, dry yet soft, parting obediently under pressure. It was the same when I drew her down beside me, the two of us lying in the thin withered grass and dust: the way she obeyed or agreed immediately; responding as I should have hoped or expected.

For various reasons, I never told him. I thought he wouldn't have understood, little realizing then how close we were, he and I, how much we had come to share. Both of us thinking black . . . or white. (Colours,

I have begun to realize, are often interchangeable; like those white Nehru shirts which, in a flow of spontaneous friendship, he had told her to make for me as well.) No, after that night it was easier to whisper to her while he wasn't watching, or to slip her short directive notes. And then, when he was asleep, only the boisterous ungovernable life of the township still wakeful, to meet her at the edge of the two gardens, at the narrow ditch which was all that truly separated the two properties.

The rains had come by then and on most nights I took her across the garden and into the house. With the other lights extinguished, the feeble lamp which burned beside the bed coaxed soft blues and purples from the sheen of her bare skin. In the almost silent room, I would watch the patterns of living colour shifting in time to our movement, until her muted cries, unexpected, broke in upon my own passionate reveries. Afterwards, only vaguely aware of her even breathing, I liked to talk: not of Europe, but of Africa, the land of the future, unsullied at last by rapine and betrayal. And still, typically, night after night, she said nothing, listening as she did during the earlier part of those evenings: expectant, ready, waiting, as for that moment when he would beckon to her, pushing the glasses across the table, mindless of the liquor which spilled on to the unstained mahogany surface.

Eventually, as had to happen, he found out. Or rather, to begin with he suspected us. There was the night he came banging on the door, his powerful voice rising above the clatter of rain on the iron roof.

"Mina, are you in there?" — the English for my benefit.

Immediately she stirred beside me and would have gone to him. Much as she responded to my voice when I called to her between the hibiscus bushes which lined the property. (A true daughter of the people. But of which people?) So, too, on that night: before I could restrain her, she actually sat up on the bed and reached for her long dress-cloth. But I wanted no midnight confrontations, and I stole with her out of the back door and into the rain.

It wasn't cold; only dark and wet, the bare earth slippery underfoot. When I heard him walking around the house, blundering in the darkness, I made her lie down with me in the narrow dividing ditch, the two of us clasped closely together in the shallow stream of water, amongst the sandy mud and sodden leaves and twigs, the refuse of the passing storm.

After the rain had stopped and he had given up and gone inside, I meant to creep out of hiding, to take her back into the house. But she was warm beneath me, totally invisible now; and I undid the pin holding her cloth loosely in place and kept her there — while in the township the vestiges of raucous laughter echoed across the night towards us.

Naturally he had guessed the truth: that it was I who was enticing her out. He was waiting the following evening. Not with the usual offer of drinks, but with a frown of outraged disapproval.

"This is not the old Africa," he said, and he held up her dress-cloth, dry now, but with patches of mud and bits of leaf still clinging to it.

I could see her, through the wide doorway past his left shoulder, going about her work in the kitchen, moving noiselessly to and fro in the deepening atmosphere of the early evening.

"It was her choice as well as mine," I said. "This is a free country after all. You've told me that yourself."

"Yes, free for us," he countered.

He spoke with such quiet assurance, such forceful simplicity, with the drums starting up in the background as the last of the daylight seeped away.

"Free!" I said scornfully. "When she's subject day and night to your slightest whim!"

"She is my sister," he said. "I have a duty to protect her from you. She is no white man's slave."

I admit now that that stung me, made me retaliate with words which should never have been spoken.

"Have you forgotten the old saying?" I flung back at him. "How the slave always makes the worst of masters."

And before I could move, he grabbed me by the shirt front (one of the white Nehru shirts which she had made for me at his special bidding) and threw me back against the wall. Instinctively, I called out her name; and as I crashed down onto the small side table, in an instant of half-suspended action, I saw her falter slightly in her work. The merest pause; no more than that.

"Now leave here," he said, breathing heavily. "This is not your place."

I stood up slowly. At first I thought that he had torn my shirt; but it was merely twisted. I pulled it straight and faced him once again, the two of us dressed identically in those borrowed clothes.

"Why don't you let her answer for herself?" I persisted.

"Mina!" he called — a single short word of command — and she came obediently and stood beside him. "You belong here," he said to her sternly, "with me, amongst your own people. This is your home, nowhere else."

"No," I contradicted him, "your place is with me. Collect your things, I'm taking you out of here."

There was a period of drum-filled silence during which the vital, undisciplined life of the township threatened to invade the room in which we stood. For a second or two, I half-turned and looked out through the darkness at the tiny jewels of fire which twinkled between the huts and trees of Shilembe. They seemed alive: minute pin-points of flaring light breaking through the deepening gloom. When I turned back to the room, momentarily they were all that I could see: small bright jets of flame flickering around the shadowy hem of her dress-cloth (indistinguishable in that poor light from the one I had scrabbled from her in the muddy ditch), fiery tongues licking at the soft warmth of her calves and thighs. But that vision lasted only for an instant, while she wavered unhappily between us. Then she raised her eyes, looked at me once, briefly, a glance of strangely mingled hatred and love, and turned away, walking slowly and dutifully back towards the kitchen.

It was not my last sight of her. Since then, I have frequently seen her shadowy figure passing across the kitchen window or carrying drinks out to Aaron and his new guests. Watching her on such evenings, I cannot help but re-enact that painful closing scene. Except that in my imaginary version, I make one uncharacteristic change, in an attempt to separate myself from him forever. Instead of that single flat statement, I say to her:

"What do you really want to do? Stay here or come with me?"

That much, a simple substitution of words, is temptingly easy to imagine. It is only the possible outcome which eludes me. What then? Do those tiny jewel-like fires (which came close to blinding me) never flicker alive in that closed atmosphere, not even for a moment, making all of this unnecessary? Or do they flare up into one purifying flame, purging her, enabling her to step free at last? Absurd questions really, because that was the one choice I never gave her.

Just the same, it's difficult not to ponder such possibilities. Especially on noisy nights, when the drums are particularly insistent and in the nearby township the sounds of fighting and endearment and laughter go on and on. Unable to shut out those familiar sounds, I sit here in the unlit room, wearing one of the Nehru shirts she made for me, and brood uselessly over those times. Though invariably with the same result: always, without exception, I am forced back to what actually happened: to how Aaron led me to the screen door of the verandah and ordered me to leave; and how the thin cotton sleeves of our identical white shirts brushed against each other (like a single cloth-clad arm and its mirror image briefly touching) as I walked indignantly past him, out into the night.

# The Empty Room

Since Emily died, I've taken to locking the door at night. Not the bedroom. I've moved out of there. Into what used to be the sewing-room — small, musty. I lie in there at night with the door locked, the room streaked with deep shadow by the tree outside. One long branch reaches out towards the window, brushing against the glass in even the slightest breeze. Tap. Tap. The shadows stirring across the floor and walls, never quiet. I keep meaning to cut if off, that limb. It makes the room airless and reminds me of him. He still comes — almost a year since I lost Emily. Tapping at the door. Are you awake, he says. I lie on my side in the narrow bed, not answering. The room is airless and hot, its blind western wall releasing the stored heat of the day. Open the door, he says, I want to talk. Just for a few minutes. I know what he wants and I remain silent. Often he pleads. Please, he says, just this once. Please my love.

He still calls it that. I did, too, until almost a year ago. His footsteps across the closed courtyard to the outside room and his footsteps up the passage to me — both of them the same in my confusion. That was why I sent her away. What was her name? Rosie, I think. Or Ruby? It doesn't matter. I wanted the outside room kept empty. The high frosted windows closed up; the sun-warped door locked — from the outside. That's important. His footsteps only in the passage, and me waiting alone on the bed, indistinguishable from the shadows. Nobody out there.

Which is why I changed my mind and took on Emily. I didn't plan it. One morning I heard a light knocking on the kitchen door, and there she was: fat, middle-aged, as black as the shadows cast by the tree — and almost sexless. Hardly a woman at all: her shapeless figure draped in a faded mother hubbard, her head bound tightly in a checked scarf. Almost impossible to imagine her a mother or a wife. The image of a thousand other ageing black women I had half seen since my childhood — both sex and character discarded somewhere in the past. She stood, I remember, with her hands cupped together across her stomach, almost protectively; yet patient, waiting for whatever I would decide. As though from that moment on, her life was in my keeping.

I never really went beyond that first impression of her; not while she was alive. The impassive unformulated face; the ungainly overweight body, round-shouldered and thick-limbed; the slow lurching comfortless walk. That was all I ever really wanted to see — an obstacle even he balked at. A kind of sleeping partner, but in a way he could never understand. So much more dependable than his promises.

I still depend on her; but differently since her death. On her silence. She never spoke very much, and then only in a murmur. Never revealed herself. For a whole year, shuffling through the background of my life, the scarcely audible sound of her bare feet scuffing the wooden floors — leaves whispering against the darkened window. Shadow and silence. Often, at night, when he comes to the door, I find myself consciously copying her — receding into the quiet; shutting out all but the sound of my own laboured breathing, the blood-heavy murmur of my own heart; reducing the whole house to the ghostly dimensions of a single unlit room. Like practising to be somebody else.

He can't stand it for long. I hear him walk impatiently down the passage, through the kitchen, and out into the courtyard; but he does it out of habit now, with nowhere to go in the middle of the night. It's different at weekends: frequently he drives to Lourenço Marques, or Mbabane in Swaziland, where he can get what he wants legally. I don't care, as long as he leaves me alone; as long as I don't have to think about what he's doing. Not because of jealousy, but because it's always Emily I imagine — young, as she must have been once; comely without ever being beautiful or even desirable. It's absurd, I know, an illusion; you can't wipe away twenty years, conjure an image that is dead and gone. Besides, I never used her in that way. Yet I did use her, as a kind of substitute — I admit that. Which is why, when I blot out the picture, refusing to see her in that role, I'm the one who takes her place — the night-dress pulled up to my shoulders, my own skin grown dusky in the half-light of the room.

It's always one of us two — never Rosie or Rachel or whatever she was called — who should be there, who fits the part. She was young and careless enough. I remember her face well. On Saturday and Sunday afternoons, when she served tea in the garden, the two of us sitting primly under the frangipani, I used to watch her, waiting for a sign between them, expecting her to smile or snigger. But she never did. I should have valued her more. Ruby, perhaps it was. I didn't care at the time. That girl's got to leave, I screamed at him, I'm throwing her out of here. He told me to go to hell — and meant it. I didn't dare defy him then, though I wanted to. Like wanting to commit suicide, but with someone standing over you, preventing violence. I had to plot my own downfall, slowly, without his noticing. It took me four months to save the money, not knowing how she would react to the idea, having to endure his late-night visits as best I could. That, too, was summer, and with the door and windows open the sounds came clearly across the courtyard to where I lay waiting. None of them cries for help. Yet when I spoke to her finally, she was quite happy about the plan. She didn't snigger at him either — simply made up some story about going home to the Transkei, ignoring his protests. In her own way she was trustworthy enough. But I held back the money until she was actually in the taxi, with her parcels and bundles piled on the back seat. A thin sheaf of crumpled notes placed on the faded leather upholstery. The room empty at last.

That, in a way, was how I kept it, right up until the hot afternoon in midsummer when I stood in the courtyard and pulled at the locked door. The peculiar disturbing smell lingering in the confined space; the heat reflected from the surrounding brick walls, rising from the slate paving. So much glare from the white door and yellow bricks that I could hardly see. She had been gone almost two days by then.

I have often wondered since what precisely it was that I missed. Because I never really knew her. Though I had chances enough. Such as the day I asked her about her past, on the farm in the Northern Transvaal, before she came to Johannesburg; and she told me about the twin boys, her first children; simply mentioned them, without comment. I should have realized — she had only one daughter still alive and I too was brought up on a farm. I know how in some rural areas the old people looked upon it as a bad omen. The mother had no choice. But I didn't want to see her in that light — neither as a grieving mother nor as a victim.

Or the first time I found her clutching her stomach as though it were alive, a faint line of perspiration gathered around the edge of her turban, from the pain. At the African hospital I spoke to the doctor myself. I'm not sure, he said, it could simply be period pains. Her Pass Book — I have it still — shows her age as forty-eight. But

I didn't try to grasp the idea. Lying in his bed, that night, I turned it into a joke. She's still a woman, I said, technically at least she could have a child. But not seriously believing it — merely something for us to laugh at; no real threat to my security.

I never took her back to the hospital; and, silent as always, she didn't once complain.

I tried to make it up to her. Twice, after she died, I asked her daughter to come here, to take her place. The second time, in a long letter in which I admitted everything. I thought I knew what I was doing — the girl so tall and slim, so different from Emily, with a young attractive body and a dark fine-moulded face. Almost beautiful. But she never replied. I'm grateful to her for that. It would have been a mistake in so many ways. A vengeance Emily never would have asked for. Also the same error repeated, though in reverse, using the daughter much as I used the worn flesh of the mother. Essentially the same disregard. Yet worse even than that — far worse. An excuse, releasing me from the suffering of his footsteps in a way I could not have foreseen. Protecting me as I never protected her, luring him across the courtyard, keeping him away from this door.

Because in spite of everything, all the guilt and hatred, I still think of him as a man. Not often; only sometimes. He always senses it, standing outside the door, persistent in his tapping and calling, his crude and childish enticements — the shadows stirring on the walls and floor, flickering over the white sheet which covers me. Ashamed, I push the pillow between my legs and grip hard, drawing its softness into me — as though my life, my womanhood, might ooze away in profane desire, leaving only a bloodless flesh husk.

Once, only once, it happened when he was in Mbabane and I was in the house alone. I was half asleep. The branch at the window must have roused me. That was the most frightening, simply because nobody was there. I had become like him. Anybody would have served. I didn't care. I clenched hard on the pillow, wanting to cry out; but with nobody to hear, the house and the room empty and still.

How much worse it must have been for her. Not just a matter of shame or desire. Her whole life dissolving, slipping away; the night unending. No greying into morning. Nobody. Until I, two days too late, stood in that heated cell of a courtyard — totally unaware, tapping at the door as insensibly as the tree against the glass.

But there was no ignoring the smell. It lingered in the stultifying atmosphere like a premonition, growing steadily with the heat of the day. By the middle of the afternoon it was unmistakable. I remember shaking the handle frantically, rattling the old pressed iron lock and hearing the key fall on to the concrete floor inside. I hooked it out eventually, somehow, and opened the door. The stench, that first blast, was indescribable — a breath from hell — the accumulated enormity of all the years I had spent with him.

I think it was the quantity which shocked me most, the sheer volume. The mattress and sheet caked with blood; a huge pool of it beneath the bed, extending out over more than half the floor — a great thin wafer of life, already dull and cracked in the fetid air. So much warm vitality, negligently squandered. Within seconds flies began buzzing in through the open door. I made myself look at her, uncertain of what I would encounter. She seemed smaller than I remembered: lying on her left side; her night-dress pulled up to her shoulders; her drooping breasts fallen on to the discoloured sheet. A pillow, dyed dull brown, the colour of earth, clay, was jammed as if by violence between her thighs. Yet she seemed oblivious of it, strangely quiet and still after the final abandonment, uncorrupted — her face calm, her legs drawn up, both hands cupped peacefully around her knees. More like sleep than death.

They didn't come for her until late in the afternoon, almost evening. I stayed with her, the two of us waiting together. A kind of belated vigil. I couldn't bear the thought of leaving her untended in that lonely room — as though I were the one curled up on the bed, watching her through half-closed eyes.

It's hard to say precisely what I saw. Her face, certainly — small, old-young, lined and girlish, with a plain slightly pug nose and full womanly lips. That was what I told him when he kept pestering, asking what was wrong, what had happened to me. Her face, I said, the person she was. But it wasn't as simple as that. A feeling as much as anything else, my own feeling at the sight of the blood, so much of it. And yet not the blood either; not that alone. The bloody female opening of her body. That also. The two together. The blood gushing between the gaping lips of her vagina, betraying her, revealing her, a kind of birth and death at once. A total revelation apparent in her last futile loving embrace of the pillow. Not the face, not the worn splayed feet, nor the sagging black flesh of her belly. The truth hidden somewhere between the clenched thighs and manifested unexpectedly in the corrupt pool of blood. More than a pool — a tide which continues to flood the courtyard, surging in broad rivulets along the passage, to lie in dark shifting stains of shadow on the floor and walls of the locked room.

I tried to follow it, as you would a river, to its source. To Soweto, the huge sprawling African township which borders Johannesburg. I had never been there before — it was like a journey into a past I didn't know I possessed. The sordid undifferentiated sameness of it was appalling — as though an unseen giant hand had reached down blindly and masked the face of its multitudinous life. Every street was identical: row after uniform row of small rectangular houses, plain brick or unpainted plaster, all with dull grey asbestos roofs. Not a tree or tall shrub to be seen. Only the skeletal shapes of the telegraph poles rising out of the bare yellow dust into the hazy atmosphere of the summer evening — like gaunt crosses, a graveyard of undiscoverable identities.

I found the house just as darkness fell. She unlocked the door in answer to my nervous knocking and motioned me inside. It was a room not unlike the one I had just left — featureless and bare. She stood in the middle of the hard earth floor, watching me, so much more obviously feminine than Emily, attractive even in the glaring light of the single unshaded bulb. To begin with, she was distant, withdrawn, her face registering nothing. But when I told her and she began to cry, the set mask of her face seemed to slip and she suddenly looked more like a child than a woman — whimpering softly, her hand and wrist curved protectively over her eyes. I waited, expecting her to stop, to ask what had happened, but she just went on crying, her breath catching in small half-stifled sobs. She never spoke. When I asked her, for the first time, to come back with me, to take Emily's place, she made no sign that she had heard. I might as well not have been there. I took out the money I had brought, that I owed Emily, and placed it on the table beside her, smoothing out the sheaf of used notes on the rough wooden surface. But they curled up as soon as I let go of them, making an unsightly heap in the crude light.

Outside, the street was sombre and deserted. I heard the key, inside, turn quietly in the lock. Moments later the tenuous thread of light beneath the door disappeared. Emily, too, had preferred the darkness — chosen it at the end — the two windows, high above the courtyard, closed and blank. Perhaps the pains, flaring up again, had been light enough for the descent of that dark river: the bleeding, initially only a thin trickle, a stream, growing at last into a pulsing flow; her heart, quickened by fear, dutifully beating out her death. Sometimes it seems that just to visualize it is to inflict it on her anew. Even once had been too much. To founder in a gulf of darkness and silence. Making no attempt to cry out, to bring help. Preferring to take refuge in the night, behind the locked door -- the courtyard as wide and arid as a desert — trusting her life, child-like, to the ineffectual comfort of a pillow; as though preparing for sleep.

I did what little I could to foster the illusion — for her sake, not for mine — because the mere act of touching her destroyed any vestiges of illusion I may have still possessed. I guessed that beforehand, which is why I hesitated, struggling with myself throughout the rest of the afternoon. But when I heard the ambulance on the drive, it was different. I didn't want them seeing her as she was. I stood up and walked across the half-circle of blood to where she lay — the dried crust crackling under my feet at each step. Lifting her as best I could, I began easing the crumpled night-dress down over her body. It was more difficult than I expected — the body set and stiff in the attitude of death, the skin cold and hard to the touch. But I managed it in time. When they tapped lightly on the door, behind me, the hem of the garment was pulled down to her feet, the pillow showing merely as a slight bulge in the cheap cotton cloth.

I let them do the rest. My hands and arms felt suddenly chilled, almost as cold as hers — in spite of the lingering heat of late afternoon.

Now, on hot summer nights, I often lie awake for hours, unable to sleep, listening. He paces the courtyard, restless, periodically stalking up the passage to call to me through the door. He is growing increasingly impatient. I'll divorce you, he shouts, leave you and this shell of a house. He's right — it seems to get emptier — the tree making a hollow tapping sound on the pane, like dry lifeless fingers. I want to live, he shouts, beating at the door, not spend my life pleading with a ghost. The door is firmly locked. Secure. I have resolved never to answer him. Through desire and disdain, I hold to our shared silence as to a pact. That much, at least, I owe to her. Yet sometimes, in the dead of night, after I have heard him sigh and settle to sleep, I wonder whether she would understand. I'm not sure. As I have discovered, it is no easy thing, communicating with the dead.

# Chiba & Son

When I received the telegram saying the old lady had finally died, I just dropped everything and took the night train to Durban. Not because she had really meant anything to me. She wasn't the kind of person you got close to — in fact she was best steered clear of. To be honest, I rushed down there in the hope that there was something for me. She'd given me damn all while she was alive; there was just the chance things would be different now she was dead. Also, as it happened, I didn't have much to leave behind me in Johannesburg.

But when I arrived in Durban in the mid-morning — the poor downtown area where she lived already hot and sticky, stinking like a fragment of old India — things didn't look too hopeful. Not at first, anyway. She'd been drinking more heavily than even I'd imagined and the house was in chaos, with dirty clothing heaped in the corners, litter and filth all over the floors, and empty bottles wherever you looked. Room after room the same. She'd really gone to pieces at the end — or very nearly. There was just one indication of sanity left, in the little box of a room she called the office. That too was filthy; but there were no bottles in there, and her account books and files were set out neatly on the grimy old desk.

At least one thing, then, had remained clear in that fuddled old brain of hers — the value of money. Which meant that in a crazy kind of way she'd gone on trying to survive; because that's what money always represented for her — life itself. She'd dinned that truth into me often enough in the years before I left home. "Everything in life has a price tag," she used to say. "You're a fool if you don't see that; and you're a worse fool if you pay more than a thing's worth."

Well I may be a fool in some ways, but even I could see that those carefully kept accounts of hers were my only chance of finding anything worthwhile in all that mess. Just the sight of the neatly arranged desk made me feel hopeful again. Without so much as opening a window to let the stench out of the place, I sat down and spent a couple of hours working methodically through her affairs.

What I found not only cheered me up: it made me respect the old girl, in spite of everything. Oh, she was broke all right; worse still, she was in debt. But she'd fixed things so the house and furniture hadn't slipped out of her grasp. Or should I say, so they hadn't slipped out of the family's grasp, because I was the only child, and they were mine now. What had happened was this: she'd realized some time before that the old man's pension was no longer enough to support her and to keep her in drink. Any normal person would have either given up drink or mortgaged the house. But she never was too much like other people. Instead, she'd sat down and worked out a system. It was dead simple really. She began by paying one of her accounts fairly regularly — it was with an Indian store called Chiba and Son. That gave her a good credit rating. Then, using Chiba as a reference, she slowly amassed hundreds of small debts all over town. She didn't pay any of those, because she made sure none of them was big enough to warrant a court action.

Maybe it wasn't a great scheme, but with her behind it it worked for a while — for almost two years, in fact, which was a pretty good run, all things considered. Like her, it only started to break down towards the end, and for the last three months she hadn't even been able to pay Chiba. With her usual luck, though, she got out in time. She never did like paying more than was necessary. She always preferred someone else to foot the bill for her.

It was that last thought which took me off to see Chiba, who at that stage was nothing more than a name to me. As I said before, I'd never had much from the old girl, and now that I'd finally got the house and furniture I didn't want any creditors making claims on the estate. It was a matter of principle, in a way. At any rate, I felt so strongly about it that I set out for Chiba's shop there and then, in the heat of the day. My idea, more or less, was to play on his feelings — the old lady's sudden death, the terrible shock and so on. It might have worked under the circumstances. I've always been a bit on the heavy side and after walking for half an hour through the midday heat, I must have been looking bloody distressed. But as things turned out, I hardly had to do a thing. Chiba did it all for me. I can see now why the old lady made him the king-pin of her system.

His shop was close to the Indian market. It was one of those rambling old general stores, dark and smelling of curry, with dusty floorboards and assistants everywhere. One of them pounced on me as soon as I walked in.

"Can I help you, Sir?"

"I want to see Mr Chiba."

"May I ask your name, Sir?"

"Harris."

He'd looked fairly cheerful until then, but when he heard who I was you'd have thought it was his mother who'd died.

"Please come this way, Sir," he said.

I followed him to the back of the shop, to a small box-like office with partition walls. Chiba was standing by his desk, inside. He was dark-skinned, almost black, in his late fifties — very short and fat, with a face too large for his body and a bulbous nose too large for his face.

"Mr Harris," the assistant announced from outside. The effect on Chiba was devastating. (God knows how he'd found out already.) His face just dropped into little fat pouches of misery.

"Ah, Mr Harris," he said.

He took one faltering step forward, stopped, pulled out a large white handkerchief, and buried his face in it.

"Terrible... terrible..." he said brokenly. "So unexpected... such a fine woman."

I thought he was putting on an act for a minute, doing what was expected of him before he gave me the business-as-usual line. But when he pulled away the handkerchief, his small dark eyes were swollen, and tears had gathered in all the fat folds of his face.

"I'm sorry," he said. "Sit down, Mr Harris."

He slumped down into the chair on the other side of the desk. He was hardly any shorter sitting down than standing up.

"This is a terrible time for you," he said. But it was too much for him and again he ducked into that large white handkerchief. I gave him a few minutes to collect himself. In the midst of all that genuine grief, there didn't seem to be any place for my small act. On the other hand, I was still red-faced and sweaty from my walk, so I suppose from his point of view I was doing my bit. He emerged at last. The handkerchief was beginning to look quite soggy.

"I'm sorry," he said again. "I heard only this morning, you understand. I am not a brave man."

I thought he was going to submerge again. But he gave his round body a shake and dabbed away the few fresh tears.

"You must forgive me," he said meekly. "I forget

even my duties as a host. You will have a drink perhaps." He called out to the assistant who was hovering just outside the door: "Bring Mr Harris some whiskey. Two, no, three bottles."

He held up three fat fingers. I don't know what he expected me to do; guzzle it down by the pint maybe.

"I do not drink, myself," he said. "But I know it helps at such times. It helped your dear mother in her sickness. 'Mr Chiba,' she would say, sitting there, in that chair, 'Nothing else stops the pain'."

It was easy to imagine her saying that. I'd heard her use the same line so many times before.

The assistant came in then, with the three bottles of whiskey, a glass, and a jug of water. He opened one of the bottles, poured out a very heavy shot of whiskey (she'd definitely been there before me), and added just a splash of water. I sipped slowly at the drink, letting Chiba have his say. He still dabbed periodically at his eyes. The handkerchief was a wet rag by now.

"Such a terrible loss for you, her son," he said almost passionately, his little fat chest quivering with emotion. "And for us all. She was an outstanding woman, Mr Harris. Outstanding."

I did my best to look simultaneously deprived and impressed.

"Yes, she was..." I groped for words, "most unusual."

"That is it, Mr Harris. For us too she was unusual. More than a customer. A woman of character. Above all," he held up one surprisingly large soft hand to emphasize the point, "above all, a fine business woman."

So that was it, I thought: he'd got round to the business angle in the end, to those three unpaid bills. But as it turned out I was wrong. He was dead serious.

He was paying her the biggest compliment his little mind could think of.

"Yes, a fine business woman," he said again. "She commanded respect — from me, from all of us."

He mopped away at his cheeks with the wet ball of handkerchief.

"It is not always like that, Mr Harris. There are many European ladies who buy from me. They come in here. Give me this, Mr Chiba; give me that, Mr Chiba. I am polite to them, always. But respect — no. She alone I respected."

"Yes, you couldn't help respecting her," I said, thinking of the old house.

"And why, Mr Harris? Because each month, when I hand them the bill, they look only at the total. They do not find out if I am honest. They know nothing of business. They look only at the total and write out their cheques. But your mother — ah, that is different. She looked at everything. 'Mr Chiba,' she would say, 'You have charged me twice for this.' Or 'This I can buy in the market for ten cents less.' Every cent was counted. She was a woman of business, Mr Harris."

He spread the wet handkerchief out on the desk in front of him, as though studying it. It didn't look as though it could cope with another onslaught.

"The whole of Durban was a shop to her," he went on admiringly. "She looked always for the bargain. Every week people would ring me, asking if her credit was good. I always told them, it is the best. Oh, sometimes they would ring again and say she did not pay. But do you know why, Mr Harris? She explained this to me herself. Because the service or the goods were bad. She was a woman of business. She paid only for what she received. Always, I said to them, she will pay what she owes. Always."

I thought I saw what he was driving at then. I was

convinced he'd get to those bills sometime.

"But I am keeping you, Mr Harris," he said. "Take the whiskey. It is yours. Please come again. Any time. You are always welcome. Remember, your mother's account here is yours. For us, they are the same."

That seemed to clinch it. From his point of view, I'd inherited more than the house and furniture. It was a case of drink your whiskey and pay up. At least that's what I thought he meant. I even felt angry there for a moment. I hadn't walked all that way through the heat for just a neat brush-off. But as it happened, I'd got hold of the wrong end of the stick once again — though I didn't realize it for a second or two.

"Look, Mr Chiba," I said, "about those three bills . . ."

"Bills, Mr Harris?"

"Yes, those three accounts which the old l- . . . which mother hadn't paid. You see, I'm a bit short right now, what with . . ."

But he waved me quiet. He looked really concerned, even hurt.

"They are cancelled, Mr Harris," he said in an agitated tone, taking a firm grip on that handkerchief again. "She was a woman of honour. She must be treated honourably. Always she paid, until the end, and then she was sick. I could see. She was shaking whenever she came into the shop. But she would accept no help. Now it is different. There is nothing to pay."

The handkerchief was useless and he wiped his sleeve across his eyes several times.

"Mr Chiba," I said, taking him by the hand, "you're a gentleman. I'd like to ask you to the funeral, but . . ."

"No, Mr Harris," he cut in. "Please do not apologize. I am an Indian. I understand our society."

"It isn't that, Mr Chiba. As I said, I'm a bit short right now and I'm not too sure how I'm going to arrange things."

I was really pushing my luck, I knew, and not expecting much of a response. But he positively jumped at the idea.

"But she deserves the best, Mr Harris, the best!" he said passionately.

And who was I to argue? So in a sense he was the one who ended up inviting me to the funeral. It was quite an affair. True to his word, he gave her the best of everything. It must have cost him a small fortune. And that's not all. Half the Indian storekeepers in town were there — including some of those she owed money to. Evidently Chiba was quite a big wheel financially, and he just leaned on anybody who'd had the slightest connection with her. He wasn't having her dishonoured even in death. We all stood around the grave, the men in their black suits, the women in sombre-coloured saris, everyone as hot as hell in the summer sun. When the coffin was lowered, I threw a handful of dirt in (which was quite appropriate in its way) and then everybody tossed petals after it. That was the minister's idea. Chiba was the only one who didn't join in. He stood to one side, working his way steadily through white handkerchiefs, one after the other, until the side pockets of his dark jacket were bulging with them.

I suppose the whole thing was a bit of a laugh really — especially if you consider what started it all. I sometimes try to imagine the old lady chuckling over it. But that's just wishful thinking, because she never did have a sense of humour. She didn't believe in gestures either. Given the chance, she would probably have argued that it proved conclusively what a fool Chiba was, paying out all that money for someone who didn't exist — who never had existed come to that.

I'm not sure if I'd have argued with her or not at that stage. It's hard to say. On the one hand I could see that he'd got everything arse about face — she would have said he'd misread the price tag. On the other hand, he had pulled me out of a hole and helped brighten up my return to Durban. And somehow the two ideas kept getting mixed up. I just couldn't see him straight. Luckily, though, I was given another chance to iron things out in my own mind — about three months later. This time it was his turn to come to me; because now he was the one who'd suffered a loss (or so he thought) and who needed a favour.

I'd settled myself into the old house by then and landed myself a job as a used car salesman. I don't think I'd given him a thought for a while. But one night at about ten o'clock, there was this godawful banging at the front door. To be honest, it put the fear of death into me because I thought it was the police. Only ten minutes earlier, I'd lured the African maid from next door into the house; and there we were in the bedroom together, she already half-undressed. I was off that bed in a flash: I wasn't too keen on being hauled off to the station on an immorality charge. She didn't grasp what was going on at first, and just sat there looking confused. But I had enough presence of mind for both of us. I bundled up her dress, shoved it under her arm, and dragged her through the house to the open verandah at the back. Before she could pull away, I half lifted her onto the wooden railing and pitched her over into the bushes below. It was quite a drop and she fell fairly heavily, I thought for a moment she might have hurt herself. But she scrambled to her feet down there in the darkness and lifted one hand up into the light. I couldn't see her face.

"Money, Baas," she said.

In certain respects I agree with the old lady — you shouldn't pay out good money for nothing. But with that thumping on the front door still going on, what option did I have? I pulled out a five rand note, which was too much anyway, and gave it to her. Then, as soon as she'd run off, I straightened myself up as best I could and went to the door.

I don't mind telling you, it was quite a relief to find old Chiba standing there. Before I could say a word, though, he ran towards me and leaned, sobbing against my chest — well, against my stomach actually, because that's as high as he reached.

"They have taken him," he said. "They have taken my son."

What could I do? I took him through to the lounge and let him cry himself out, his face buried in one of those white handkerchiefs of his. He didn't drink, so while I was waiting I had one for him. I needed it in any case. Only when he'd quietened down did I try to get any sense out of him.

"Now tell me slowly," I said, "exactly what's happened."

"My son, Raj, they have taken him."

"Who's they?"

"The police, Mr Harris. The Special Branch. They have arrested him."

I didn't like the sound of that, especially after my recent scare.

"Did they take him away from the house?" I asked.

"No, Mr Harris. He just disappeared five days ago."

"Then how can you be sure he's been arrested?"

"Because I feel it. Here!" he said, punching himself feebly on the pudgy chest.

"But that isn't enough, Mr Chiba. How can I help you unless you have more proof than that?"

Of course, that's the last thing on earth I should have said to Chiba. I'd already discovered how ready he was to think the best of everybody.

"Ah, Mr Harris," he said. "I knew you would help. I

said to myself, with such a mother, he is the man to go to."

"But Mr Chiba, you still haven't told me what proof you have."

He looked furtively round the room, almost as though he expected some Special Branch men to leap out on him.

"I trust you, Mr Harris," he said softly. "I tell you the truth. My son Raj is a student at the Indian College. For more than a year now he has had many political friends. What do you call them — left wing. I said to him many times: Raj, forget about politics. It does no good. Study your economics and accountancy; pass your exams and come into business. It is the business which matters. But he would not listen, Mr Harris. And now he is gone. Five days ago he disappeared."

"And you think the Special Branch have nabbed him?"

"What else, Mr Harris? I know my son. He would have told me if it had been anything else."

It all made sense: I had to admit that. And there had been talk of recent arrests in and around Durban.

"So what are you going to do?" I asked.

"That is why I come to you, Mr Harris."

"But why me?"

As you may have gathered, I had a very real respect for the police force and wasn't anxious to become involved with them.

"Because I am an Indian, Mr Harris. If I go to Pietermaritzburg, to the Central Station, they will not even listen to me. And I am not a brave man. But you are a European, Mr Harris. If you speak politely to them, they will let you see him perhaps, speak to him, find out if he is well. That is all I ask, Mr Harris. To know that he is well. To be sure that he is not badly treated."

That was the amazing thing about Chiba: he was

absolutely serious. He genuinely believed that I'd go to the rescue of his blessed son, that I'd start tangling with the Special Branch for the sake of someone I'd never met.

"Look, Mr Chiba," I said apologetically, "I know I owe you a favour..."

"Favour?" he asked, puzzled.

"Yes, the old lady's funeral and everything."

"No, no favour, you owe me nothing, Mr Harris." He waved the idea aside. "Everything I did was for your mother. For her sake. It is I who ask the favour. Out of friendship. That alone."

That gave me the lead I needed.

"Out of friendship, Mr Chiba, I'd gladly help you. You know that. But it's more than a question of friendship. I have other responsibilities." I vaguely indicated the rest of the house, as though it were bursting at the seams with dependants. "There are other people who rely on me. I have to think of them as well. What would become of them if I was involved... if anything happened... You follow me, Mr Chiba? I'm sorry. I really am."

I thought it was a fairly clear-cut refusal. But as always he interpreted it in his own peculiar way.

"Please don't apologize, Mr Harris. I understand. There are times when business and friendship are no longer separate. When they are the same. Your dear mother, she understood that also." He reached inside his jacket and pulled out a cheque book and pen. "It is right you should protect those you love. It is for the same reason that I come to you."

He sat there, trusting as hell, his pen poised above the open book, waiting for me to name a figure.

"I put myself in your hands, Mr Chiba," I said.

I felt I could rely on him as far as that was concerned. I was right, too. He scribbled away for a minute and handed me a cheque. It was... what shall I say? Substantial. You couldn't call him a mean man.

"Don't worry any more," I said. "I'll do everything I can. You have the word of a friend on that."

So there I was landed with the problem of what to do. Don't get me wrong: I had no intention of marching into a police station and demanding to speak to Raj Chiba. I'm not that stupid. On the other hand, having taken the cheque, I did feel called upon to make some kind of gesture. (That, incidentally, is just one way in which I'm different from the old lady.) I thought about it for the rest of the evening and most of the following day. I finally worked out a solution late in the afternoon. It was a compromise really. I decided that the least I could do was actually go through to Pietermaritzburg. Not confront the police. Just visit the town. I couldn't do any good, I knew that. But it would show the right spirit. It would give Chiba the idea he was getting something for his money. And that, after all, had more than satisfied him in the past.

At six o'clock, then, when we closed up the shop, I borrowed a big Chev from off the floor and shot through to Pietermaritzburg. It was a fifty-five mile run on a multi-lane highway, and less than an hour later I pulled up outside the Central Police Station. That's not as stupid as it may sound, because directly opposite the police station is the Imperial Hotel. My idea was to have a few drinks, a good dinner, and after that drive home. But you know how it is: two drinks become four and so on. And by about ten o'clock I was good and plastered.

I don't remember the middle part of the evening too clearly. But I know that towards the end I was standing at the bar arguing with three characters I'd never seen before. For some reason I haven't fathomed, I was trying to convince them that there were Indians in Natal who were the equal of any white man in the country. "Fine men," I kept saying. "And great business brains. I'd trust them with my life." Needless to say, you have to be careful who you tell that kind of thing to, even in Natal. You certainly don't go spouting it out in hotel bars. All things considered, I suppose I got off quite lightly. There was no fight. What happened was that one of them upended a jug of iced water over my head, and as I stepped back, with the shock of it, I skidded on the ice cubes and fell flat on my jack. You can imagine the laughter that caused. And I couldn't do a thing, not with three of them against me. I got up and staggered out into the foyer, absolutely fuming.

Now from the foyer of the Imperial Hotel, you look straight across to the flight of concrete steps that lead up to the main entrance of the red-brick police station. And at the sight of those steps I suddenly developed this crackpot notion. It came to me as clear as crystal, the way things sometimes do when you're drunk. Chiba had paid me to help him and that's what I intended doing. My word was my bond. I'd show those bastards in the bar. I was going to walk up those steps and demand the release of my Indian friend. "It's a matter of honour," I said to the old chap who was sitting at the desk.

Fortunately for me, my luck took a turn for the better at that point — otherwise I would probably have made a fool of myself. As I stepped out into the street, my eyes fixed on those steps, a police van swung out of the side entrance of the station and came gunning down the street like a bat out of hell. The driver picked me up in the lights only at the last moment, swerved madly, and just squeezed past between me and the kerb. It was bloody close, I can tell you. I swear the off-side fender touched my trouser leg as it flashed by.

That sobered me up all right — brought me to myself as it were. And with the silly ideas knocked out of me, I saw immediately what I should have done all along. I went straight back into the foyer of the hotel, to the public phone, and put a call through to Chiba. He answered it himself.

"This is Harris, Mr Chiba. I'm ringing from 'Maritzburg."

"What is happening, Mr Harris?"

"They've attacked me, Mr Chiba."

"Attacked you?"

"I tried to get in there and they attacked me."

"You are all right, Mr Harris?"

"I think so. I'm not sure. But there's nothing else I can do now. They've warned me not to come back."

"You have done enough, Mr Harris. I am truly grateful."

"I could perhaps try again."

"No, Mr Harris. It is too dangerous. You must leave there now."

He sounded really concerned for me, and also impressed, which was just as well because Raj was found two days later, hiding away in the home of some distant relatives, thirty miles up the North Coast. It wasn't a political affair at all. He'd fallen in love with the daughter of one of the top intellectual Moslem families in Durban — her old man was a school principal, and her brothers and sisters all doctors and lawyers and god knows what else. But her family had made it clear that the wedding wasn't on. They weren't having her marrying into a crowd of Hindu storekeepers, no matter how rich. The Indian community is like that in Natal. Very traditional. Anyway, young Raj just went to pieces. Couldn't face the thought of life without her. Reckoned his heart was broken or something. With not so much as a word to anyone, he crept off up the coast. Threw up his studies and everything. All he wanted was to be alone, so he could mope and pine away. If you ask me, it was rather like one of those bad romantic movies — the kind the Indian and Pakistani studios turn out by the dozen.

Naturally Chiba was delighted to have the boy back. When he rang me up to tell me the full story, he could hardly contain himself. The marriage, he thought, could be arranged, in spite of the opposition. (He was probably right — money can accomplish most things in the end.) In the meantime, he wanted to have a party, to celebrate the return of his son. He asked me if I'd go along, as guest of honour. The idea quite appealed to me — I'd often wondered how the other half lived.

So on the following Saturday, I dressed up in my best gear, stuck some plaster on my face to give the impression I'd had a rough time in Pietermaritzburg, and set off. Chiba had a place in the plushy part of an Indian area called Reservoir Hills. It was a three storey affair, all in white stone, with a flat roof and two domed towers in the front. Just looking at it put my mind completely at rest about that cheque he'd given me. Obviously, his business interests extended way beyond the general store.

He met me himself at the front door and introduced me to everybody. Young Raj, as you might expect, wasn't up to much. He was one of those slight, soft-featured young fellows, almost beautiful, more like a girl than a man. I suppose his being so miserable didn't show him off at his best. He stood there in the corner, looking as though he was going to burst into tears at any minute. When I was introduced to him, he shook my hand feebly and said how grateful he was for all I'd done and how sorry he was for what had happened to me. But his heart wasn't in the words. It was just talk. You could see he was thinking of that girl of his, wherever she was.

Everybody else enjoyed themselves, though. Chiba

bounced all over the place, nearly bursting out of his black suit in an effort to be the perfect host. And most of the men stood in small groups, talking business as hard as they could go. I spent most of my time chatting up the women. You should have seen some of them — fantastic creatures, with near perfect features, and wearing enough jewellery to float a sizeable company. Just being with them started me feeling randy, and I made a mental note to get in touch with that African maid again. Not that you could seriously compare the two — there just didn't seem much point in wasting the fiver I'd been fool enough to hand over.

Towards the end of the afternoon, to round things off, there were a few speeches. Raj apologized for all the anxiety he'd given the family, and Chiba said how grateful they all were to me and what a friend I'd been in a time of trouble. I even said a few words myself — how close our families were, seeing eye to eye on so many things, and how, under the circumstances, I'd done only what you would expect. As far as I was concerned, it brought everything to a satisfactory conclusion.

When I finally left, both Chiba and his son saw me to the door.

"Once again, Mr Harris, we must thank you," Chiba said.

Raj stood behind him, sullenly, not saying anything.

"That's all right, Mr Chiba," I said, looking meaningfully at Raj. "I just hope you don't need to call on me again — for your own sake."

"Ah, no, Mr Harris. We have come to an agreement, Raj and I. I have said to him: give up politics. That can help nobody. Pass your exams and come into the business, and I shall persuade the girl's family. They will agree to the marriage. I have promised him that."

"You listen to your father," I said to Raj. "Devote

yourself to the business. Get that idea straight in your head and everything else will be easy."

He didn't look particularly thrilled with the advice.

"There," said Chiba admiringly, "there speaks the voice of wisdom."

Which of course was going too far, but then Chiba never did practise any moderation.

We shook hands and I climbed into the car. But I hadn't gone half a mile before I realized I'd had a couple of drinks too many. And if there's one thing I feel strongly about, it's drunken driving. There's not enough respect shown for human life on our roads. So I put her into third gear and toddled along at thirty. I don't believe in taking chances.

Travelling slowly like that gave me time to ponder a few things, and it suddenly struck me that the party, like the funeral, was a bit of a laugh in many respects — because neither event really had much to do with the actual situation. I think it was then I decided that on balance the old lady was right: Chiba was more of a fool than anything else — goodness knows how he made so much money. Basically, he was a confused man. And in spite of her many faults, that isn't something you can say about the old lady.

# Part II

Part II

# Refugees

We received news of the convoy late in the afternoon, my father standing with the phone in his hand, his habitually gentle expression touched with pain and surprise. My mother was immediately against his becoming involved: she said it would only encourage trouble from across the border and bring violence onto ourselves as well. He listened to her quietly and attentively — that was always his way. But finally her arguments made no difference, and we went together, he and I.

I was just fifteen then and it happened shortly before I, too, became part of the migration south. I remember we collected Laban and Joseph from the compound — they were also father and son, yet entirely different in appearance and character; as different in many respects as my father and I. They crouched in the back of the truck, out of the wind, as we bumped down the dusty farm track. At the main highway we turned north, towards Mufulira and the Congo, travelling more quickly on the tarred surface; speeding through the brief twilight, the bush indistinct on either side of us; only the short isolated trees of the savannah standing out black and clear against the pale dusk-yellow sky.

The convoy had already arrived when we reached the Mine Club. I had vaguely expected to find French cars, Peugeots and Citroens. Instead, there were mainly American models, Buicks and Dodges and such like. They were parked in a long row out front, the heavy overhanging fenders coated with brown dust, the roof-racks and seats piled high with luggage.

My father wanted me to wait outside. He said there

would be a time for me to witness such scenes, in later years, when I was older. He wasn't, as I have since suspected, uttering any prophecies: it was merely in his nature to be protective — not only of me. But I went with him anyway. Partly out of curiosity, partly because I didn't wish to be left behind with Laban, rejecting even then that possible identification.

They were all inside the Club, seated around the edges of the central ballroom. They looked more tired than frightened, though some of them, men as well as women, were crying quietly. Others were leaning forward, their hands covering their faces. The two whom we had agreed to lodge for the night were in the far corner: a woman and a young girl about ten years old, sitting close together. As we approached across the smooth wooden floor, they stood up: the woman blonde and quite young, with a pale vacant face — I don't mean innocent, not that — simply empty, as though nothing existed behind the inexpressive mask of her features. The little girl was different: her face tense and drawn and somehow wrinkled; more like the face of an aged monkey than that of a child, the knowing, experienced eyes peering out at you.

I can't remember what was said. I think we hurried them out of the Club, away from that atmosphere as quickly as possible. They were both of them quite calm at first, until we reached the truck and Joseph jumped down to take their luggage. Then the little girl shrank back against her mother and the woman shouted out:

"Don't let him come near me!"

I didn't understand that at the time, the undiscriminating nature of her horror. Now, removed in space as well as time, having since shared her ignominious journey, I am more able to savour the bitter taste of her simple half-truth. But not then. It would have been understandable to me had she rejected Laban in that way; but it appeared senseless where Joseph was concerned.

He stood beside the truck, hurt and confused, unaware of what he might have done.

"*Bwana?*" he said, puzzled, "*Bwana?*"

Appealing as always to my father who quickly stepped between them, his back to the woman.

"She's upset," he said. "She doesn't know what she's saying."

He was standing very close to Joseph, both hands placed reassuringly on his shoulders, caught as it were in a single frame of memory: a grey-haired white man, tall and slight, and a short muscular African; set apart from each other by age and race, yet so similar by nature.

It was only a momentary difficulty and minutes later we were travelling back to the farm, the woman seated between us with the child on her lap. Outside it was completely dark, just a faint suggestion of dusk still visible along the line of the horizon. Inside the cab, the illuminated dashboard cast a greenish glow onto the wrinkled monkey face of the little girl and brushed the pale cheek of the mother, making her look more like a corpse than a living woman. I glanced over at the speedometer, at the unsteady needle which measured off the miles — the first of the many which I was to share with those strangers whose names I cannot even recall. None of us spoke very much. Yet it was some time during that short trip that my father told them how my mother and I had also decided to go south. "It's too dangerous for them here," he said, telling it as though it were his own decision rather than ours, the sound of his voice, peaceful, without trace of resentment, perfectly clear to me after all these years. The woman put both arms around the child, drawing her close.

"Where else is there to go but south?" she said.

It wasn't really a question. While behind us, Joseph

and Laban watched through the back window of the cab, staring past us, at the apparently solid walls of tall yellow grass lining the road.

She spoke a good deal more later, after we had eaten. Perhaps she felt more secure once the servants had gone. Or it may have been my mother's kindness towards her — I've never seen her more considerate to anyone, as though she also saw in the woman a dim mirror image of herself. But whatever the reason, the woman suddenly began speaking of the past, of her experiences in the Congo. That was what I'd been hoping for all along, with the cold-blooded curiosity of the young. My father, however, interrupted.

"Peter," he said quietly, addressing me formally, so I knew I couldn't refuse. "You go off to bed now. This isn't for your ears."

In my own room, I lay quite still in the darkness, listening to the drone of her voice, to the way it mingled with the cold insect noise of the night. For a while I dozed off; but when I awoke she was still speaking, and I got up and crept silently down the passage.

The door was slightly ajar and, crouched there invisibly in the deep shadow, I could see through the narrow frame of the opening the back of my father's head and, over his left shoulder, the unnaturally old face of the little girl. The woman herself was out of sight, but her voice reached me clearly:

"He wouldn't leave. It didn't matter how often I asked him. He said it was his duty to remain. His duty! To stay there in that filthy hole of a hospital, working for people who resented his very existence. Not really people at all — more like animals. Probably the same ones who only hours or days earlier had been trying to kill us. All smiles now, in the clean wards; all friendliness because they were sick and needed him. I told him that, but he wouldn't listen. Not even after we lost Stephen."

There was a murmur of sympathy from someone in the room, probably my mother. Within the narrow opening of the door, the old intent expression of the little girl didn't alter.

The voice continued:

"He said it made no difference. His own son and it made no difference! Leaving won't bring him back, he said. That was when I decided to get out. All around us people were leaving, packing up their cars and driving south. And I still had one child left to save." A hand appeared and stroked the round exposed skull of the little girl. "I told him, I'll wait for you in South Africa; you'll find us there when you come to your senses. I wasn't going to lose her the way I lost Stephen."

"What did happen to your son?" My mother's voice again.

"He was outside the house, with the nanny... in broad daylight... and they... they..." She faltered, and for a moment there was complete silence. "It's hard to talk about it now," she went on. "He was just an innocent child. And that black bitch ran off and left him. A baby. All alone. All alone out there."

My father was sitting right forward on his seat, temporarily blocking the daughter from view.

"But why was there nobody with him?" he asked, the words slightly muffled, as though he found them difficult to articulate. "Was there nobody to protect him?"

"Could I watch over him every minute of the day?" Her voice hard now and defensive. "Didn't I have another child to worry about as well?"

And then the daughter's face appearing again, thrust upwards and forwards, contorted with the same hard impenetrable quality as in the mother's voice.

"They waited till he was all on his own," she said shrilly.

My father made no attempt to reply, though as I now appreciate, what he did was answer enough in itself. He stood up and turned away from all of them, towards the darkened, half-opened doorway, to where I crouched invisibly in the shadows. It was not, of course, an appeal to me: he had no means of knowing I was there. Still, I often feel compelled to interpret it in that fashion. It was the way he looked: not really changed; his face merely drawn into a more intense likeness of itself, of the man he truly was — his actual expression almost impossible to describe.

That wasn't the only time I saw him so affected. There was one other occasion, which I have since learned to recall with disturbing ease. It happened a day or two before the arrival of the convoy, barely more than a week before we were due to go south. I had driven with him to the far edge of the property, beyond Stony Ridge, to where Joseph was working alone, digging a well. He was still down there when we drew up: in the abrupt silence we could hear the dull regular thud of the pick, the sound, muffled by the depth, like the slow peaceful measure of a heartbeat. My father went to the top of the wooden ladder and peered down into the cool darkness.

"Joseph," he said quietly.

The work stopped and after a few moments Joseph climbed up into the light. He was stripped to the waist, his young sturdy body, almost perfectly black, dappled with tiny drops of sweat.

"Any sign of water?" my father asked.

All around us the bush lay hot and still, burned to a uniform grey-brown by the months of drought.

"Water come soon now, *Bwana*," Joseph said confidently. "I dig little bit, little bit. Maybe three feet."

He bent down, indicating the depth with his hands.

"Are you certain it's down there?" my father said.

"Sure, *Bwana*. I find him." He laughed with pleasure at the idea, as though the water were already there, moving under his hands, transforming the inert dust at his feet. "Six feet, *Bwana*, plenty water." He spread both arms wide, inundating the shallow valley in which we stood.

"How much is plenty?" my father asked, laughing with him.

"Much water, *Bwana*. I smell him."

"Enough for the cattle?"

"Sure, *Bwana*." With a single wave of his hand he dismissed the visible farm — the dry earth and charred scrub. "Plenty for grass; plenty for trees; plenty for cows. Many fat cows, *Bwana*." Like a child, he blew out both cheeks in playful imitation of the cattle he imagined. "The *Bwana* will be rich," he said innocently.

"All right," my father said, still laughing, "next week you can come back and make our fortune."

In fact, Joseph probably never did complete the digging of the well: too many other things intervened. On that particular day we drove him back over the ridge to the farm compound, a double ring of mud huts built some distance from the house.

Normally, at the sound of the truck, children came running from the compound, begging my father for a ride. But that afternoon nobody came to meet us. The whole area seemed deserted, not even a village dog anywhere in sight. Parking the truck next to one of the narrow patches of vegetable garden, we walked through the two lines of huts to the clearing at the centre of the village. The people were all congregated there, old and young alike, grouped into a silent, watchful circle. In the middle of the circle, standing alone, was Laban, his flat hard features as unyielding as ever; and next to him, docile and unsuspecting, an ageing black and white bull. As we reached the edge of the crowd, Laban raised a short wooden-shafted spear and thrust it into the bull's side, just behind the right shoulder.

I had never seen a ritual killing before, but I knew immediately what it was — the way Laban pushed the spear in only so far and then released it and stepped back, with everybody waiting silently, watching to see what would happen. The old bull didn't fall: it merely staggered slightly and afterwards stood quite still, the muscles of its shoulders quivering, its large clear eyes staring innocently at the assembled crowd. Probably it was too badly injured to move. Yet that was not the way it appeared. For perhaps a full minute it seemed almost untroubled, almost totally at peace. Only when it finally tried to walk did its true state become apparent. It took one staggering step, then its gaunt body convulsed, and as it toppled forward onto its knees, two red streams flowed out of the dilated nostrils, down over the broad black muzzle. For a moment I thought it would fall right over: the hindquarters swayed dangerously, while the head, twisted sideways, actually touched the ground. But somehow it managed to recover, slowly straightening one leg after the other, heaving its great head clear of the earth. Not until it was standing once again did the crowd stir: a barely audible rustle of movement, as though an idle breath of wind had brushed the edge of the village. In the forefront of the crowd, the young children, almost naked in the afternoon heat, stared patiently at the injured beast. It looked stricken now: its whole body leaning at an angle; its legs peculiarly bent. From where the head had touched the ground, the cornea of one large eye was coated in dust, as was one side of the black bloodstained muzzle. Two slimy threads of red saliva trailed from the corners of the mouth.

I half turned away, intending to go back to the truck and wash my hands of the whole affair, but my attention was caught by an odd choking sound right beside me. It was my father, his normally tanned skin gone completely pale.

"Laban," he said quietly, his voice strangely altered, "that's enough."

Laban was standing casually beside the dying animal, his heavy arms hanging loosely at his sides. He paid no attention to my father's voice.

"D'you hear me!" my father said more loudly. "I told you, that's enough!"

Laban turned his head slowly. It was the first time he'd shown any consciousness of our presence. But even then he did nothing: merely stared at us, his eyes small and bloodshot.

"For God's sake finish it!" my father nearly shouted.

And still Laban did nothing: just went on staring at us coldly. I think by then my father was the only one still watching the beast.

"Come on," I said, tugging at his arm.

But before I could pull him away, Joseph shouldered his way through the crowd, grasped the spear with both hands, and drove it further into the animal's body. The creature must have died instantly, because it toppled sideways from the force of the blow, its head stretched out, all four legs rigid. Joseph, unable to regain his balance, fell forward into the dust, one hand sliding on the slimy patch of blood and saliva. After that I couldn't see what happened to him, because the people started to clap and cheer, the children leaping up onto the side of the still warm body.

In all that noise and commotion nobody paid any more attention to us. For them, I suppose, it was a kind of victory. Even Laban had looked away, as though nothing had happened. Only my father remained exactly as he was, his face unnaturally pale, wearing an expression which at the time I did not understand.

"Come on," I said, again urging him to leave.

But all I could make him do was turn around. He wouldn't come with me. He stood there looking fixedly at the mud wall of the nearest hut, his gaze unwavering, as though he could perceive the significance of the whole event in the dust of those crumbling mud bricks. Eventually, when he wouldn't come, I left him alone and went back to wait by the empty truck.

I almost forgot the events of that afternoon, and also that particular picture of him. They came back to me years later, long after his death, when I was working as a press photographer in Johannesburg. It was the time of the trouble in Mozambique and I had been sent to the railway station with one of the reporters to meet a refugee train from Lourenço Marques. It wasn't the first such train I had met. As it came in there was the usual crowd of relatives standing on the platform, staring anxiously at the passing carriages. And the refugees themselves were not noticeably different from others I had seen: some of them angry; many of them weeping and pale-faced. I wandered through the crowd taking shots while the young reporter I was with questioned various groups. He, as far as I remember, was more disturbed by it than I. As we left the station, he said: "Someone will have to answer for this."

Yet it wasn't his remark alone which really distinguishes the experience of that day from other similar occasions. It was what happened afterwards, back at the paper.

I was working in the dark room, developing the shots I had taken, looking out for those which would best capture the events of the morning. One after another, the isolated faces took form and shape in the shallow pans, floating up to greet me in the present. I had expected them to be characterized by deep emotion, by grief or heartache, even revenge. But suddenly that was not the way they appeared to me. There, alone in the strangely revealing half-light they looked merely lost, their vacant or bitter eyes touched by a quality of bewilderment, like so many aged children lost in a strange land. Each frame like a window into the past. Nearly all of them the same. Only one exception: a man of indeterminate age, half turned away, as though looking back to where he had come from — the face locked in shadow.

I knew then that we had been mistaken. And that evening I drove across town to see my mother. She lived in a high-rise flat in the northern suburbs and was always urging me to visit her more frequently.

"Peter!" she said, surprised and pleased to see me, and she kissed me lightly, her skin dry and brittle to the touch, a wisp of permed hair rasping lifelessly across my passive cheek.

"I'm going back, mother," I said.

"Back?" she asked, puzzled.

"To the farm."

She could hardly believe what I was saying.

"But you can't," she said. "Nobody's there now."

"He's still buried there."

"What difference does that make? There's nothing you can do for him any more. There never was anything you could do to help him. It would have happened just the same, whether we'd been there with him or not."

But I could no longer take that view, and a month later, having resigned from the newspaper, I began the long journey back; travelling by road once again, as though the earlier journey could somehow be annulled.

It was a revealing trip. Once north of the Limpopo, I didn't rush things, stopping frequently to photograph the thornscrub or the flat dry savannah. Peering through the lens of the camera, concentrating on the land itself, on deliberate square portions of grass and trees and sky, I methodically tried to recapture what I had lost: the quiet calm atmosphere of the bush; the farm where I had been born and had grown up; the house I had finally left. It was intended as a slow, deliberate process of rediscovery — almost as a reawakening. Except that like those silent images which had floated up from the shallow pans in the dark room, it was not exactly what I had expected. Because always, at every moment of every mile — whether standing on the sand bed of some vanished river, or crouching in the long grass, fingering an outcrop of grey limestone — always, the landscape around me remained unmoving, oddly deserted, as though I were moving deeper and deeper not into the living past, but into the dry hot land of the dead. Even the people who stood by their huts or watched at the side of the road as I drove past appeared strangely still to me, their loose waving hands blown listlessly by the wind of my passage, their faces and bodies covered with fine brown dust, like crumbling statues dissolving back into the earth. Wherever I looked I received the same impression of lifelessness, the same still, frozen quality, which the brief bustle of Bulawayo and Salisbury could do nothing to dispel — the hot afternoons and the black starlit hollows of the night disturbed only by the thin metallic whir of insect life. Everything became like a vacant image of the past, dead and unpossessed, my own fixed and vanquished memories somehow travelling before me, reaching out and stifling the hidden, inaccessible vitality of the countryside.

So that long before I actually reached the Zambezi, I had begun to realize that there could be no real return; that whatever else the journey might have been, it was no more a return than our earlier deliberate withdrawal had been a flight. The past and the present congealed into a single immovable sequence.

Ironically, and perhaps justly, it was the Zambian authorities who gave substance to my growing awareness of failure, by refusing to allow me to cross the border without a visa. The official who interviewed me at Chirundu, on the Zambezi, was very polite, but quite firm in his refusal. He was dressed in immaculate white, his shiny black skin and gentle face disturbingly reminiscent of Joseph — a more effective custodian of that distant farm and its silent occupants than even I could have envisaged.

I didn't try to argue with him. Nor did I begin immediately what was in fact to become a kind of flight. Instead, I travelled a few miles back up the escarpment, as far as a dried-out watercourse, and then turned off the road, driving slowly between the trees, bumping across the uneven hillside, until I reached a blunt spur or promontory of rock which jutted out over the valley. From there I could see the whole sweep of the Zambezi — the river running between yellow and green banks, split at intervals by gashes of white sand — and beyond the distant shoreline, the steep, tree-covered hills of Zambia rising up to meet the level grasslands of the plateau which stretched up to the north, to Mufulira and beyond.

I remained there until the evening of the following day, hidden from the road by the curve of the hill, too far above the valley to be visible from below. During the long night I crouched before a small fire until the mosquitoes came out in force, and then took refuge in the car. By day I clambered up onto the outjutting rock and sat there in the hot sun, peering across at the distant hills. Again, nothing seemed to stir. As the second day wore on, the far thickly wooded slopes changed slowly from bright morning green through into shades of heavy purple, the shadowy folds shimmering slightly in the late afternoon heat. From time to time small dots moved across the sand to the water's edge, their progress almost imperceptible, like hands on a watch, but they were too far away to identify as living creatures, animal or human. I might easily have been the only living thing for miles around. Yet in spite of the distance and the stillness, I didn't feel totally removed from those steep slopes. Perched up on the dry rock, it was at least possible to imagine the live forms moving slowly through the thick forest or sauntering warily down towards the water which separated us.

I packed up the car at dusk, carefully stowing away my now useless photographic equipment in the boot. In the deepening shadows I drove to the road and, without looking back, began the long return journey. I had very little to show for my brief and rather belated effort — in many ways my mother had been right. And yet not completely so: because at some point during those long hours I spent on the rock, peering out across a now unbridgeable gulf, I discovered the truth about my father's death, the actual circumstances under which he had died.

It happened not long after we left. He awoke one morning just before dawn, totally alone in the house, and heard the sound of firing over beyond the ridge. As he dressed and hurried from the house, he must have remembered my mother's constant admonition to take a gun with him. But his Quaker beliefs, as well as his natural disposition, must have made that unthinkable; and, as always, he went empty handed.

They were stealing the cattle that had been left to graze the valley around the unfinished well, firing off guns to drive the reluctant beasts quickly into the scrub country beyond. It doesn't matter now who they were — tribesmen from across the border, perhaps, or even some of the local people. Nor would it change anything to discover their motives — whether they viewed his arrival with hatred; or whether they merely saw in him an image of the white man and reacted out of fear, thinking that such a person would not come unarmed. The one certainty is that as he stepped from the truck, they shot him through the chest and he fell immediately.

The sun had risen by then and was showing just above the horizon. He was lying in the faded grass on the lower part of the slope. Moments after the yellow sunlight touched his cheek, they dragged him across the narrow valley floor and pitched him down the unfinished well.

Miraculously, he survived both the shot and the fall. Throughout the early part of the morning he lay in the soft mud and stared up through the dark tunnel at the diminishing circle of blue and at the delicate puffs of grey-white cloud which hurried faster and faster across his line of vision. He was still alive when, later in the morning, Joseph and Laban came looking for him. It was Joseph who climbed down into the darkness. After the brightness above he could see very little; but he could hear quite distinctly the breath bubbling in the throat of the dying man.

"*Bwana!*" he said, his voice echoing the expression which I had twice perceived on my father's face.

When he received no answer he stooped into the dark mud, lifted the helpless man, and climbed with him to the surface — that alone, a feat which defies any rational explanation.

Typically, Laban stood indifferently to one side, refusing to take a portion of the heavy burden until Joseph, near the end of his strength, strained unsuccessfully to lift the dying man onto the back of the truck. Only then did he step forward and lend a hand. And it was at that moment that my father vomited up a quantity of blood and died. Joseph was still holding him close when it happened and the blood flowed down over his right hand and arm.

While Laban went off to ring for the police, Joseph remained beside the body, clutching his own stained flesh and crying. He didn't try to wipe off the blood. Why should he have done? We, after all, were twelve or thirteen hundred miles away: someone had to take the responsibility; and, like my father, he was in one very special sense alone.

Of course it might be objected that I had no way of discovering the events of that morning. As I have already said, I failed in my attempt to return to the farm; also, I have neither seen nor heard from Joseph since I left there as a boy. It might seem, then, that this account is merely surmise.

Given the choice, I would gladly concede that point. But unfortunately the felt truth of those distant, unseen events goes beyond all reasonable doubt. Like a thin strip of wound film, it springs into life at the slightest touch, flickering vividly across the passive screen of the mind. No mere illusion of lights and shadows.

It is not my only such experience. Shortly afterwards, during the Angolan crisis, I read about the refugees who took to the boats and journeyed slowly southwards. And immediately I saw them with the same vivid certainty: black and white crammed together in a motley assortment of craft, all floating hopelessly on the uncertain sea, unable to land. Nothing happens in this particular picture. In the foreground, on dry rocky promontories, stand the giant figures of white officialdom, their grotesque bony legs forming crooked archways through which I look out onto the ocean, at the directionless boats and lost souls who crouch within them.

Again, I was not there to witness those scenes for

myself. By then I had come to recognize my own true status and had finally crossed those seas upon which they perpetually flounder. Here, now, sitting at the window of my room, I look out onto the Australian landscape which is not so very different from the Africa I knew: the same yellow winter grass; the stunted gum trees easily mistaken at a distance for the twisted knobthorns. Yet the resemblance, so striking at first, is really only superficial. Beyond the limits of this actual scene, the boats ride endlessly on the surf — the faces, black and white, haunted, peering over the sun-blistered gunnels, like reflections in a mirror. And beyond them again (a single negative overlaid by several images), that final glimpse of the farm.

My father is lying in the truck in the hot afternoon sun. I can no longer see his face, only his feet and the lower part of his legs which jut out over the tailboard. Near by, bareheaded in the strong light, stands Joseph. His hand is still stained with the vomited blood he is guiltless of; and he is crying, his face puffed and swollen with grief. To the right of the picture Laban is sitting in the shade of a large jacaranda. His face is unaltered, merely slightly older, reminding me of the ten year old girl who once spent the night at the farm — the same dark and peering intelligence. Both men are staring at the house as at the lens of a single eye, their gaze fixed on a point where I cannot choose but stand. Neither of them calls out or makes any visible sign. They merely stare: Joseph with a hint of accusation; Laban with a faint cold smile of recognition.

# Part III

Part III

# The Traveller

It is obvious that he is a stranger, that he doesn't know Sydney, by the way he walks in no particular direction. Aimless, wandering through the late afternoon crowd. His curiosity carefully veiled.

At one point he stops in the doorway of a bar, hesitates, then descends the carpeted stairs. Down below it is noisy, smoke-filled. And also vaguely familiar. On his right, two women are talking together. He leans closer, waiting for a possible opening.

"So I told him the truth," she says — the young, attractive one — "that he's a pakeha bastard."

He recognizes then the faint air of familiarity. Maoris. More of them at the end of the bar.

"And did he know what you meant?" he says, trying to sound friendly, almost confidential.

The woman looks up. Heavy eyes; wide, curving nostrils. Very nearly beautiful.

"What?" she says.

"The pakeha bit." Smiling carefully. "What did he make of that?"

"Oh, you a Kiwi too?"

Her voice perhaps slightly drunk.

"I lived there a couple of years," he says. "Before that in Africa. I've only been here two weeks."

The Africa part is included for effect. Exotic. But she ignores it.

"Two weeks is long enough," she says. "You've seen what it's like here. Because we're New Zealanders, they think we don't know anything."

He nods patiently and orders drinks. Paying no attention to the plain, silent girl beside her.

"They take us for a crowd of country bumpkins," she goes on. "Especially me. I'm just a jumped up black to most of them."

Listening to her, he realizes that she is barely aware of him. Filled with her grievances and nostalgia. He lets her talk, knowing that's the only way. Not until she's on the point of leaving does she really notice him.

"Well, time to go home."

Stubbing out her cigarette; pulling the strap of her bag up on to her shoulder.

"Do you have to?" he asks. "Couldn't we make an evening of it?"

She looks at him then. Lowers her eyes.

"I mean," he adds, "we're both from New Zealand. Travellers you might say. I just thought . . ."

"I'm sorry," she says, "I've already made arrangements."

She turns away, embarrassed; but immediately hesitates, almost guiltily, half-remembering something said earlier.

"You've only been here two weeks?" she asks.

"That's all."

Another hesitation.

"Look," she says, acting on impulse now. Scrabbling in her bag for paper and a ball-point. "I know what it's like being stranded in this town without friends. If you need someone to show you around, give me a ring."

After she has gone, he smooths the used envelope out on the bar. On the back is scrawled the name Marion, followed by a phone number and an address on the Cross. He carefully folds the envelope and slides it into his top pocket. Still smiling, but differently now. Pondering the curious question of pity as he finishes his drink and climbs slowly up towards the street.

When he arrives back at the house in Coogee he finds that Nora and Jeff have delayed dinner for him.

"How did you get on today?" Nora asks as soon as he enters.

She sounds anxious, her forehead puckered with concern.

"Oh for pity's sake, Nora!" Jeff cutting in. "Give the man some peace. You don't have to grill him every time he comes back."

"I'm not grilling him. It's just that I know how bewildering Sydney can be to a stranger."

"If you ask me, you're the only stranger around here, Nora."

"Now, now," he says, silencing them both. Placing a friendly hand on each of their shoulders. "I don't want you quarrelling about me."

He finds it odd, their constant bickering, not sure of quite what it signifies. It is forever breaking out. He can't even go to bed without an argument. Later that evening, Nora says:

"I'm amazed at you, Jeffrey. Leaving your study in that state. Books and papers everywhere. How do you expect him to sleep in those surroundings?"

"Damn it all, Nora, he only sleeps in there. What does it matter once the light's out?"

"It's the idea. Nobody likes sleeping in chaos."

"Who the hell knows what they like when they're asleep?"

He sidles out and leaves them arguing. Because the truth is, he doesn't particularly care either way about the room. If anything, he prefers it slightly the way it is — unopened cartons of books piled up along the wall, the temporary day bed wedged between the desk and the filing cabinet. No sense of permanence. Lying there at night, he feels he might be anywhere. Even back in Africa.

But Jeff raises the topic of the room again next morning.

"I'm sorry about the study," he says guiltily. "It was bloody thoughtless of me. I'll clear it up a bit this afternoon."

"And about time too!"

Nora's voice from the kitchen.

"I said I was sorry didn't I?"

"Being sorry isn't enough. People need more than your sorrow and your pity. They need a little care."

There's no stopping them, he thinks, and escapes onto the verandah. Watching the Saturday morning traffic churning past the house.

But at 10:30 he takes the folded envelope from his jacket and goes to the phone. Marion herself answers, her voice heavy with sleep.

"Who is it?" she asks suspiciously.

"It's the fellow you met in the pub yesterday. You said I should call you if I needed someone to show me around Sydney."

"Yes . . . " Hesitant, puzzled. And then suddenly remembering: "Oh yes, I know."

"Well, as it's such a marvellous day . . . "

Another hesitation.

"Well . . . I suppose . . . yes, all right. Why not?"

"Good, I'll pick you up in half an hour."

As he puts down the receiver, he senses someone standing in the doorway behind him.

"I didn't mean to pry," Nora says apologetically.

And Jeff's voice from the sitting room:

"No, it's second bloody nature by now."

She takes him to the places he has already been to — the opera house, the art gallery, the botanical gardens. He says little, apparently content to be shown around; but all the time he is watching her, waiting for the right moment. He finds her features almost savage now — the broad cheekbones, the flared nostrils, the short, curved upper lip. And her light brown skin, smooth and foreign, reminds him of the past. Yet he avoids the obvious comments which might easily be misinterpreted. Carefully biding his time.

She is distant, withheld. Almost official in the way she explains the places to him. Not until late in the afternoon does she begin to relax. They are crossing the harbour on one of the ferries and she is leaning on the rail beside him.

"It must have been a marvellous stretch of water," she says, "before they fouled it up."

There is in her voice the same quality of resentment and regret which he had noticed on the previous day.

"Not like the Manukau harbour in Auckland, is it?" he says, wondering if that is what she wants to hear.

"Oh that!" she says. "It's nearly as bad as this place."

"Where's better?" he says softly, trying to read her mood.

"Lots of places. Bay of Islands. The Marlborough Sounds. The Sounds especially. We used to go there when I was a kid. About five miles from Picton. Not another house in sight. Just our little cottage and a stretch of water like this. The hills all green, covered in bush."

"Will you ever go back?" he asks.

She shakes her head as if shaking off the mood or the memory.

"No, you can't go back. Not like that."

Standing away from the rail. Looking impatiently towards the shore.

He hunts quickly for a way of recapturing the more intimate mood.

"Yes, a harbour like this holds memories for me too," he says regretfully.

"In New Zealand?" she asks.

"No, Africa." Pausing as he tries to recall the names of harbours. Lourenço Marques perhaps? But all he can remember are the brothels and the plates of prawns on the tables of the outdoor cafés. "Durban," he says vaguely, "Beira, Lourenço Marques, Walvis Bay."

He notices with relief that they are just names to her.

"And you miss them?" she asks, the suggestion of concern in her voice reminding him suddenly of Nora.

"Worse than that," he says resignedly. "It's knowing that you can never go back, never go home."

Home, he observes almost with amusement, has become several different countries, but she shows no signs of disbelief or doubt.

"Never?" she says, leaning towards him.

"I'm the wrong colour," he says. "I'm not lucky like you." Reaching out and stroking the soft brown skin of her hand. "There's no place there for people like me."

"But that's terrible" — more like Nora than ever now.

"And it's not only the place that you miss. That's bad enough. But there's also the people. Those you love."

"A woman?" she asks gently.

He nods, trying hurriedly to separate the faces, the many smooth brown bodies — all of them darkened by memory.

"She wasn't well educated or anything," he explains, "so they wouldn't let her come with me. In any case, she couldn't leave her village, her people, everything."

Distant views of thatched villages, in the bush or on the open veld. Hastily recalled. Barely noticed at the time. His attention always held by the road.

"Then you'll never see her again?"

"Never."

Final. No plea. The simple flat statement all that is necessary now.

"My God!" she says, placing her hand on his arm. "And I think I'm hard done by. When all I have to do is spend three hours on a plane and I'm home."

"It must make you feel secure," he says, "wanted."

"And you in this brute of a country all on your own," she murmurs, "with no going back."

There is no need for him to make any further effort after that. The idea of his exile fascinates and touches her. The simple image of two people separated by the gulf of space and colour.

All through dinner she questions him about the woman — her background and personality, what she is doing now, whether she feels isolated and alone. He plucks details from his past, resorting to invention whenever necessary. Only her name he withholds, on grounds of sentiment.

That single omission seems merely to inflame her curiosity. Back in her tiny flat, after he has kissed her, she says:

"But what does she look like? I mean, her actual appearance."

"She's much darker than you," he says. "Otherwise very similar."

"Really like me?"

"That's why I was drawn to you yesterday."

"Similar in what ways?"

"The same lips," he says, kissing her again. "The same soft brown skin" — slowly unfastening the buttons and slipping the blouse from her shoulders.

She offers no resistance. Allows him to undress and

lead her to the bed. Merely, at the critical moment, saying once again:

"Really like me?"

But he doesn't bother now even to answer.

Afterwards, she still can't leave the idea alone.

"You're a refugee," she says. "D'you realize that? Not like me. I'm just a traveller. Away from home for a spell. But you're a real refugee."

He nearly tells her then, what has been in the back of his mind all along. That it doesn't matter where you live; how countries aren't very different from each other. None of them a home. Or all of them perhaps. But he checks himself, knowing now what she wants to hear, and says instead:

"It's often worse for those who remain behind. With no one to comfort them."

"Yes, comfort," she says, snuggling warmly against him, "we have that" — preparing herself for sleep.

He too sleeps for a time. But in the early hours of the morning he wakes, looks at the room in the dim light coming in from the street. The walls are covered in posters and prints; candles and incense over the fireplace; shells, books, knick-knacks on the narrow shelves. All so lived in. So arranged for permanence in spite of her discontent and talk of home. He finds it impossible to rest any longer in such surroundings and slides noiselessly from the bed.

When he is almost dressed, she wakes. Rolls over and stares at him with her sleepy, heavy eyes, almost accusing in the poor light.

"Why are you going?" she asks.

"It's the people I stay with," he explains. "They'd be shocked if I stayed out all night."

"You weren't just creeping away?"

Doubtful, on the verge of hurt.

"Of course not. After finding you like this."

"Then I really do remind you of her? You weren't lying?"

"Look," he says, taking a used envelope from his pocket, the one she gave him in the bar, "if you haven't heard from me by half-past two, give me a ring and we'll make a date for tonight." He writes six random numbers down quickly. "It's in Bondi, where I stay," he says, placing the envelope on the bedside table.

Kissing her lightly on the cheek before he steals out into the chill morning air.


Nora and Jeff are pointedly tactful when he gets up later that same morning. They say nothing until lunchtime. Then Nora finds it impossible to remain silent any longer.

"We were so glad . . ." she begins.

"Nora!" — Jeff's voice interrupting, sounding a warning.

"No," she goes on hastily, "I'm not prying. Really. I just want to say how glad we are that . . . you're settling in. Making friends and such like."

He reaches over and puts a hand on hers. Affectionately.

"I understand," he says. "You're both very kind."

Even Jeff is visibly mellowed.

"We're only too pleased to help," he murmurs, embarrassed. "Anything you need now or in the future. A job, a place of your own. Anything. Not that we want to chase you out. This is your home as long as you please. You know that."

He is glad that Jeff has given him the opening.

137

"Actually, I've been meaning to talk to you about that," he says. "I've decided not to settle in Sydney just yet. Thought I'd have a look elsewhere first. Travel round for a bit. Nip up to Brisbane, or down to Adelaide. Maybe even shoot across to Perth. Just for a while."

They both exchange puzzled glances, but nothing more is said on the topic, and after the meal he retires to his room.

With some surprise, he notices for the first time that Jeff has tidied it up. All the cartons stacked in one corner, the desk and the top of the filing cabinet cleared. It appears much barer, less used. Even more restful, he decides, lying down fully clothed on the bed.

Gazing at the blank cream walls, he thinks idly back over the previous evening. Decides that it was right, what he'd nearly said — that all places are really the same. And people, come to that. Africans in a village; this Maori girl. As universal as suffering itself. Who said that? Where had he heard it? He tries to recall the speaker . . . gives it up. It doesn't matter. He knows that the only real experience is that first passionate seduction. Swift and final. The world his oyster. And yet she'd called him a refugee. He smiles contemptuously and composes himself for a nap. Allowing the two images of black-brown skin to merge into one. Finally into the silence of darkness. Sleep.

Outside the study, Nora's voice, until then only a background murmur, rises in indignation.

"And don't I deserve some consideration too? I live on this planet as well, you know."

Jeff's reply, more muted.

"Yes, but why this particular part of it?"

"That's typical of you, isn't it? You don't care about anybody but yourself."

"If that was true, I wouldn't be here arguing with you now. Would I? Well would I?"

Momentary silence. While miles away, in a distant part of Sydney, a phone begins to ring in an empty warehouse.

# Flash

There's no point in letting on now — about who finally got to her, I mean. Besides, french letters have been known to burst, in which case we're all as innocent as lambs. And anyway, Eileen was a bloody fool to bring her into the house in the first place. She was always doing it: getting these girls from some kind of reformatory outfit and giving them work in the boarding house. Keeping them off the streets, she called it. But with Flash she needed her head read: the girl was just about an idiot. Couldn't cope. Never realized what was going on, that she was being made fun of. So fucking dim that it took her about a year and a half to understand even the simplest joke.

You could see it in her face, how thick she was. We all spotted it, the very first evening Eileen introduced her. We were sitting round the table waiting for our evening meal — me (unemployed), Bob (a student), and Dave (always broke, writing some book or other).

"Boys," she said, "this is . . . " — I forget her real name now.

But I can remember the evening clear enough. Big motherly Eileen, as bright and sharp as you please; and right next to her, poor little Flash — round-shouldered, flat-faced, her skin like a nutmeg grater, pasty and red in blotches, and with those stupid mongol-looking eyes. Like someone out of a nuthouse.

"Say hello to the boys," Eileen said.

And she opened her mouth in a sort of empty smile, but all that came out was a little frothy dribble of spit.

It was during the first meal that she got her name.

She was so bloody slow, with that shuffling walk of hers, that we'd already started calling out things like "Come on Flash". But what made the name stick was what happened when she was serving Bob. She had this low-cut blouse on and as she bent over his plate she bulged out over the top.

"What you got there then?" Bob asked, and pulled at the top button — which promptly came undone, and I swear to God her little skinny right tit damn near fell in the soup.

"Just a flash in the pan," Dave said, quick as you please.

And from then on we couldn't call her anything else.

That joke also set the tone for the future. We could never really take her seriously. And pretty soon it was more or less usual to have a laugh at her expense. It wasn't difficult. She fell for just about anything. Like the time we sent her off to the corner shop to buy some holes to put in washers. The bloke who ran the place was a bit fed up with us that first time and sent her back with a rude note. But later on he joined in the fun. For instance, when we asked her to buy some left-handed cups, he carefully explained to her that he had only right-handed ones.

"But it's left-handed ones we want," Dave said, turning all the cups round on the table so their handles pointed to the right. "We've got plenty of the other kind."

"You should be ashamed of yourselves," Eileen said disapprovingly, standing in the kitchen doorway.

But really there was nothing to be ashamed about. Poor old Flash didn't have a clue. Just smiled in that dumb dribbly way of hers and was quite happy to go off to the shop and try again. What's more (can you believe it?) she came back as pleased as punch with six plain white cups.

"He says they're unberdickstroos," she said.

But probably the best gag of all was with Percy on the top floor. He was a right poof, nancying around the place in all his swinging gear, and always trying to smuggle some butch boy friend or other into his room.

"Hello gorgeous," we'd call out.

"You're insensitive," he used to say to us.

And just to prove him wrong, we began to work on Flash.

"Percy's crazy about you," Dave would whisper to her. "Dreams of you up there in that room of his. Imagines you're in his bed screwing the arse off him every night."

"He never," Flash would say, but flattered just the same, her flat stupid face grinning slyly.

"You know why he never tells you? Never gives you a touch or anything?" Bob this time. "Because he's shy. Thinks you'd laugh at him."

And then Dave again: "Put the poor bugger out of his misery, Flash. Creep up there one night and slip into his bed. Don't say anything — just get in between the sheets with him."

Which is exactly what she did. Crept up the stairs in the nude, late one night, groped her way across the darkened room, and climbed into bed. What the poor bitch didn't realize was that Percy already had some dirty old man in there with him. Well you'd have thought that the fucking house was coming down — shouts and screams and Christ knows what else. By the time we all ran out, Percy's bloke was already downstairs struggling into his trousers; Percy was on the top landing swearing vengeance on all us "insensitives"; and Flash was sitting on the stairs, starkers, giggling and crying at the same time.

The whole thing was exactly like some comedy turn on the TV of the future and we could hardly believe how successful we'd been. But Eileen was furious. There and then, she made us go down to the dining room where she gave us a good talking to. Not that we took much notice. That was Eileen's way. Her mind was like those big droopy tits of hers — warm and motherly, ready to care for every lame duck in sight.

What I liked about her, though, was the fact that she wasn't a prude. Not even where Flash was concerned. Let me give you an example. Saturday evening was always Flash's dancing night. Dumb as she was, she'd always manage to find out about some run-down dance or other and head off there. All powdered and painted up and dressed in her best gear. Not exactly a sexual delight, but a bit of an improvement on her weekday self.

And it was then, on those Saturday nights, that Eileen showed her true quality. Always, before Flash left, Eileen would take a couple of french letters out of the locked sideboard drawer and slip them in the girl's handbag.

"If the necessity arises," she'd say, waving her finger in front of Flash's dull button eyes, "you take care to use them." And then to us. "It's no use trying her on the pill — you could never depend on her to take it every day. It's much better this way."

"But why only two?" Dave asked her one time, with a grin. "Why not three?"

"Yes, wouldn't you like three, Flash?" Bob said.

"Don't you listen to them . . . " Eileen began protectively.

But before she could finish, Flash surprised us all, not only by answering promptly, but by actually making a joke — to my knowledge, the first of the only two jokes she ever made.

"That would be greedy," she said, giggling and leering at us across those flat, rough-skinned cheeks.

And greedy is one thing Flash wasn't — she was simply regular. Like clockwork, in fact. Every Saturday night without fail she'd hook some near-sighted bastard and bring him back for a weekly bash. Not in the house, like a normal human being, but as you might expect, in the narrow alley at the side of the house.

There wasn't much room there and most of the time the concrete was cold or damp. So she took to having it on the metal dustbins outside the back door. Three of them there were, all in a row, and she'd sprawl out on those for her medicine. Not that you could see her down there — it was always too bloody dark. But you knew what was going on, because sometime early Sunday morning you'd hear those dustbin lids clanging out their rhythm.

As often as not one of us would open a window and yell down — either encouragement or curses, depending how we felt. But Eileen disapproved even of that sort of interference.

"Leave the girl in peace," she'd say. "She's doing no harm. Let her have her little pleasures."

I'm not sure now what got us plotting again — Eileen's disapproval or the constant clanging of those lids. But it was after some months of those weekend performances that we came up with our final plot. Not overnight, mind you. We mulled over lots of other ideas first — pretty basic most of them, like dropping crackers or flares or water into the alley while the show was on. But all these possibilities were pushed aside when Dave put forward his suggestion.

As I mentioned, he was a would-be writer and forever scribbling or reading books. Well he told us about some Russian novel (not communist or anything) where a bunch of blokes find this dirty, ugly, idiot woman who's blind drunk and wonder whether it's humanly possible to fuck her — you know, whether they can imagine her as sexy long enough to get a hard on.

I think we all saw the point straight away: Flash was ugly enough for ten; none too clean (even on Saturdays she only dabbed scent over the smell); and as thick as two bricks. You really had to strain to remember she was female.

But Bob, who was a science student and never satisfied unless he investigated every angle, stalled for a bit.

"So what happens in the story?" he asked.

"I'm not sure," Dave admitted. "Someone screws this girl. That's certain, because she has a kid. But I couldn't work out whether it was one of the blokes who originally wondered if she was screwable."

"And you reckon we should think about having a go at Flash?" I said, because that was obviously the idea. Dave nodded.

"But what do we get out of it?" I asked. "Just some macho kick or something?"

"No, don't you see?" Dave burst out. "It's a challenge — to your manhood if you like. People are always going on about how far-fetched books are. Well here's our chance to put one to the test. We can find out for ourselves whether life ever measures up to art."

"Yes," Bob murmured, "a kind of experiment."

They were always going on like that — about art and life and experiments and other sorts of crap. It didn't mean much to me, all that theoretical stuff, but I must admit that the idea of a challenge had a certain appeal. Living on the dole as I do most of the time, you don't encounter too much in the way of challenges.

"It's worth thinking about," I muttered — and Bob and Dave nodded.

That was all. We didn't make any firm agreement and we didn't talk about it again. But I'm bloody sure we all found it attractive in a weird sort of way. I don't mean the thought of screwing Flash — God forbid! But the kind of challenge it offered.

And there, I suppose, it's best to draw a cover over proceedings. It's useless raking up a lot of shit when no good can come of it. Because in spite of all our thinking (rising to meet the challenge, you might say) there was something that at least one of us forgot — and that was the simple fact that Flash only ever had skins on a Saturday night. I suppose it's an easy enough mistake to make these days, when even fourteen year old Sunday school teachers take the pill. But there you are. Some clever prick (one or more?) crowded Flash in that alley; and in just about the time needed to rattle a dustbin lid, Flash was in the family way.

The other two never even found out what had happened. Long before Flash began to swell up front, Bob was off home up country, and Dave moved on to God knows where — probably to write another one of those unreadable books of his. Personally I'm not a family man or a traveller (in my experience sons and travellers sooner or later get landed with jobs) and so I was left behind to watch over things.

There wasn't much to do during that waiting time, though I did think back over things a bit. But who the hell can be sure about what's going on inside a woman's gut? Also, there's no one to say some flimsy piece of rubber hadn't given the game away. I know it says on the packet that they're electronically tested, but even modern materials can take only so much, and some of those dancing types are fucking fit — the long drawn out racket in the alley some Saturday nights made that clear enough. Well there's one possibility for you. And faced with that kind of uncertainty I didn't see any point in stirring things. I just kept my mouth shut and watched as Flash got fatter and slower — if that was possible.

About the only thing I found out in all that waiting is what a hell of a long time four or five months can be — especially when the main entertainments are Percy's love life and Eileen going on and on about how abortion is a sin against life. She was really strong on that — the anti-abortion thing. Wouldn't hear of Flash being defused.

I've often wondered whether she went on feeling that way afterwards. I should have asked her. Because when Flash finally did fall due, there wasn't any blue-eyed bouncing baby. Instead, after a long and painful labour, she gave birth to a mongol kid, with a cleft palate, a hole in its heart, and what the hospital called pulmonary complications. It was a wonder it survived at all. But not for long. It struggled on for three days in intensive care and that was that. All over.

I thought then that Flash would come back, and every morning I half-expected to see her come shuffling in from the kitchen. But she didn't appear, and it turned out they wanted to keep her in the hospital for observation.

"Is there something wrong down below?" I asked Eileen.

She shook her head.

"Then what the bloody hell is there to observe in Flash?"

Those Florence Nightingale types always amaze me.

"It's her attitude," Eileen explained. "She's confused about it all. Needs time to rest. That and a few old friends around her. You should come along one afternoon."

And d'you know, I let myself get talked into it, dragged off on one of those flower-carrying exercises.

I can't say it was a thrilling experience. To be honest, I preferred the other end of the proceedings — with those dustbin lids thumping out their message down in the alley. But there I was, in this tiny little private ward (which it turned out Eileen was paying for) grinning across at old Flash.

She looked bloody awful. Her skin all pasty and dead — just the cheeks still red — and her little button eyes staring out through a greasy fringe of hair.

"You're looking great," I said, trying to cheer myself up and knowing she could never resist a bit of flattery.

But this time it had no effect on her.

"Have you seen 'im?" she asked me.

"Him?" I said. "Who's him?"

Eileen, meanwhile, was waving frantic hand signals and making shushing noises with her big lips. But I wasn't having any of that.

"Come on," I said, "who's him?"

And the nurse, standing next to the bed, turned away from Flash and mouthed the word baby.

"D'you mean she thinks the kid's still alive?" I nearly shouted.

"That's enough," Eileen said. "Keep quiet."

"I'll be buggered if I will," I said. "What, stand here and not breathe a word, while you two jolly her along with a bunch of lies!"

I could never bear that kind of two-faced crap.

"Don't you think she's had enough truth for a while?" Eileen said — really cutting.

But I wasn't going to be put off that easy. I'd fooled Flash myself, when the boys were in the house, but this was different. And I marched straight up to the foot of the bed.

"Listen, Flash," I said, ignoring all the protests. "There isn't any kid. It couldn't breathe properly and its heart stopped beating. The kid's dead. And if you ask me it's better off that way."

She didn't take it in straight off. Just looked at me blankly for a minute. But the penny dropped eventually. I could tell by the way she peered slowly round the room, exactly as if she was searching for something. But you know what those private wards are like — bare as the bloody antarctic. Real snob outfits. Not even a friendly face to look at.

"Dead," she said, only the once, her voice as flat as that poor bloody face of hers.

"My poor darling," Eileen said, smoothing the greasy hair away from her forehead. "My poor darling Flash."

I was already heading for the door by then, but I was stopped by her voice from the bed.

"Flash?" she said, a question this time.

And it was then that she made what you might call the second joke of her career — at the very least she got the point of one of those earlier jokes, months earlier.

I glanced back and she was looking straight at me. Not sad or anything. Quite the reverse. She put her podgy, bitten little fingers up to her mouth and giggled.

"Flash," she said again, "Flash," looking at me slyly now, out of the corner of her button eyes, the way she'd once looked at Percy. "I know," she said. "I wasn't quick enough, was I?" And she giggled again. "I was too slow."

"Hush now," Eileen said gently.

But I grinned back at her and nodded. She'd got the idea.

# Quaker Wedding

I suppose I'm not what you'd call the confident type, which is probably why I was never sure where I stood with Anna. I could never quite get her straight. One minute I'd have this picture of her as someone aggressive and tough as nails; and the next I'd see her as gentle and innocent, everything you could wish for in a woman. It's always been like that with us.

Like that night some years ago now when I took her home after a party. I wasn't drunk or anything, and I don't think she was either. But her folks were out somewhere, so we start to kiss and cuddle a bit in the kitchen. And you know how it is — one thing leads to another, and before you know where you are...

But hold on a minute, because this is the difficult part. I mean, what happened — it's difficult to be really sure about it, to be able to say, this is exactly the way it was. All I can do at this stage is tell you what I thought was going on.

To go back to that night. I've got her up against the wall in the dark and pretty soon she begins to pant and claw at my clothes, just as though she can't wait another second. "You bastard," she says, kind of sighing, "you brutal bastard." Still clawing at me. And I reach under her skirt and drag her pants down to her knees. I'm pretty worked up myself by then and I can't really hear what she's saying any more. All I can think of doing is getting her over to the kitchen table and pulling my own trousers down. But I've no sooner done that (laid her out on the laminex top and pulled one leg clear of my strides) than I hear this noise outside.

"Who's that?" I ask her.

And before she can answer, the door opens, the light clicks on, and there're her parents standing watching us.

It's all so quick that I don't know what to say. Not that it matters, because she doesn't give me a chance.

"Get away from me!" she screams out — to me, not them. And then to her parents: "For God's sake get him off me!" Helpless now, both arms held protectively across her tits.

Well, that reaction, coming on top of her parents' unexpected arrival, has me so confused that I can't move. I don't know who to start apologizing to first. And the next thing her father has me by the collar, slugs me one in the eye, and without even giving me time to climb back into my trousers, kicks me out the back door.

I tell you, I was bloody pissed off. That bitch, I thought, and vowed never to go near her again.

But a week later I hear this knock on the front door of the flat, and there she is, looking exactly like the injured innocent.

"What the hell do you want?" I ask her.

"Your poor eye!" she says, reaching out to touch my bruise.

But I pull back, fending her off.

"You've got a bloody nerve," I say, "coming here like this after what you've done."

"After what *I've* done?" she says, sounding really surprised.

"You heard me," I say — though already (and as usual) I was beginning to feel slightly less confident.

"Isn't it a case of what you were trying to do?" she says quietly, with just a hint of accusation in her voice.

"Only with your encouragement," I insist.

"What?" she says. Exactly like a little girl now — shocked and gentle and injured all at once. Impossible to see if she's acting or not. "Are you suggesting I was encouraging you that night? You surely can't think that being raped on the kitchen table is my idea of romantic love."

"You didn't take much getting on to that table," I say, really starting to falter now.

"Does that surprise you?" she asks. "It was so unexpected. I'd trusted you until then. And besides, you know I'm not an aggressive sort of person" — which at that moment, with her wearing her most innocent expression, sounded true enough.

"So it's all my fault," I grumble, stalling for time and racking my brain for arguments.

But why go on? The point is, the more she talked and looked at me with her clear blue eyes, the less sure I became. What the hell did happen that night, I began asking myself, which one of us really lost control? Was she leading me on with all that clawing of hers or trying to fend me off? And for the life of me I couldn't tell any more.

It was never any different with Anna. There was that time she went off for the weekend with Ken, who used to be a friend of mine. The official line was that they'd gone on some kind of religious retreat. But I didn't swallow that shit. After I'd given Ken a good thumping I went round to have it out with her.

"It was perfectly innocent," she says the moment she sees my face.

"What!" I shout. "You refuse to go away with me — doesn't matter how often I ask you. Then you hike off with that lecherous bastard and expect me to believe it's innocent."

"You shouldn't judge everyone by yourself," she says gently, which really stops me in my tracks.

But as I said earlier, why bother to go on? I could never argue with her for long without feeling all mixed up and unsure of myself. Only half-convinced, you might say. There were times when she made me feel I didn't even know myself — like sharing the inside of your head with a stranger. That was what I disliked most of all. That feeling. And in the end I just gave her up. It was easier that way.

I don't mean I didn't see her at all — but only in passing. Lovers without being lovers, she called us once. And that was good enough for me. A sort of distant friend. In fact I hardly exchanged twenty words with her, for a year or more, right up until the night before her wedding, when she rang up and invited me to the ceremony.

"Please," she says, "for old time's sake."

I wasn't clear what she meant by that.

"Does Ken know you're asking me?" I say suspiciously.

"No," she says, as cool as you please, "but I'm certain he'd agree. Neither of us wants to carry any unpleasantness over from the past."

Well I thought I had her there for a while. Calling me behind Ken's back — quite bare-faced about it. Pretending he'd agree, when all she was trying to do was collect her old conquests around her on her wedding day. Gloating. Really two-faced if you ask me.

At any rate, that's what I thought at the time. Which was why I expected a flash affair. You know, dazzling white dress, bloody great church, all the pomp and show. But when I drove half-way across Sydney the next morning I was in for a bit of a let-down. For one thing, I couldn't even find the place at first. I parked the car and walked around looking for a cathedral or something; and then I noticed these people gathered outside this flea-bitten red brick barracks. And that was it — a Quaker meeting house.

I remembered then, something about Ken being a

Quaker. And it was just as the idea crossed my mind that I saw him. Standing near the entrance, meek enough for ten, with that bloody awful I-love-the-world expression on his face. And right next to him, looking more saintly than ever, was Anna. I must admit, her get-up was a knock-out. No white dress or anything. Cleverer than that. Just a plain grey frock — a mixture between the little girl and the early pioneer type, all simple and home-spun. Even her hair-do fitted the image. All that blonde hair pulled back enough to make her look sort of demure. But not too strict. Some of it left loose, falling gently about her cheeks, to remind everybody how much there was of it.

As usual she must have spotted me first, because she had that sweet butter-wouldn't-melt-in-my-mouth smile all ready for me as soon as I set eyes on her.

"I'm so glad you could come," she says, trying to take my hands. "I wanted as many old friends as possible to share this with us."

"Oh come on, Anna," I say, "who do you think you're kidding? Remember who you're talking to."

I get a few belligerent looks for that. But not from her. She just gives me that smile again and straight away the confidence starts to drain out of me. So much so, that I beat a retreat while I could and escaped into the hall.

Everybody else started to pile through the door about then and pretty soon there was quite a crowd inside. I didn't know what to expect. There was no altar or cross or anything — only the rows of chairs and the bare hall. Ken and Anna sat up front, on the right. And on the left was another couple, youngish, but with Quaker stamped all over them. They weren't there to conduct the ceremony though. As the young bloke explained to us unbelievers, there wasn't going to be anything like a normal ceremony. All we had to do was sit around until the spirit or something moved Ken and Anna to stand up and make a declaration of marriage. We could pray or think or look out of the window — do what we wanted. Even stand up and address the crowd if we felt moved to.

As soon as he'd explained all this, most of the heads went down. Anna's too, just for a minute or so. Then she glances up again, those blue eyes of hers, delicately fringed with lashes, all fresh and dewy, like something out of one of those misty make-up ads — almost too good to be true.

Under normal circumstances I'd have probably sat there thinking what a great actress she was — or at least suspected it was a pose. But to be perfectly honest, that hall or the atmosphere in there or something had a peculiar effect on me. And the longer I sat there, the more I had this creepy feeling that perhaps I'd misjudged her. I don't only mean the night before, but all along — even that time in the kitchen.

What made it even worse was the speeches. I know it must sound silly, but all that talk began to wear me down. Especially the way it harped on Anna's purity and innocence, on how she'd escaped the grubby paws of the world. Meaning me, of course. And try as I might to resist it, I couldn't stop this idea growing on me — that she was somehow blameless, and that I was as guilty as hell.

What rammed the point home was the speech of one old man — a really old bloke who creaked to his feet near the end. Like everyone else he sang Anna's praises. But that wasn't all. One or two things that he said really sank in. Like the bit about responsibility.

"Don't think for a minute," he says, looking slowly round the hall, "that you've come here today just to witness a marriage, because there's no such thing as an onlooker. What these two young people are, what they will become, is partly the responsibility of all their relatives and friends. You," he says, looking straight at me, "every one of us — we're all here today to make a decision and to search our own consciences."

Normally I don't go much on that heavy stuff, but right then, I don't mind telling you, my own conscience was giving me a bugger of a time. No matter how much I wriggled and squirmed inside and made up excuses and arguments, I couldn't help feeling that everything that had happened in the past was my fault — that Anna was as innocent as she looked, as everyone said she was. I don't think I've ever had such a strong feeling. Almost a temptation in its way. And finally I just gave in to it. Still sitting there in the hall, looking at Anna's face all peaceful and pure, I say to myself: All right, so I'm the guilty one. It was me who tried to rape her on the kitchen table and who beat Ken up for nothing after that weekend — and so on, going through every one of those past memories. And d'you know, the moment I admitted it all, that I was the aggressive bastard who was always fucking everything up and that Anna was blameless, something really weird seemed to happen. A kind of religious experience, I suppose you'd call it.

Suddenly everything looked dead simple, not heavy or complicated any more. It was exactly as if I'd cracked the secret of the universe. Unreal. If Ken hadn't got up right then and started saying how he wished to marry Anna, I think I'd have been on my feet making a full confession. Taking it all on my own head and leaving Anna free, as clean as a whistle. As it was, I sat there about a foot off the chair, just hovering, with all the uncertainty, all that bull-shit and confusion behind me. This is it, I kept thinking, the truth. Just like that. Coming to me in a flash. While everything in that hall, Anna included, seemed to sparkle and shine.

What's more, I didn't lose the feeling when we filed

out. For the rest of the morning I seemed to float. It was such a great sensation that I didn't even want to talk to anyone. I was quite content to stand on the edge of the lawn, near the back of the garden, and watch everyone else enjoying the reception — which is not at all like me. Usually I'm one of the first in, grabbing what I can before it's all gone. But not this time. Don't touch it, I thought, don't spoil anything. Leave it in peace for a change.

And I did, almost until the last. But shortly before Anna and Ken were due to leave, she waves and signals for me to come over. So I saunter up and let her take my hands in that pure way of hers, not saying a word. Stay out of it, I keep thinking.

"Have you forgiven me?" she says. "Aren't you glad now that you came? I know I am."

And she leans forward with her eyes closed, mouth pursed and ready, while Ken looks on, blank as ever. Well I hesitate for a few seconds, but when she doesn't move I finally bend over intending to give her a cool brotherly kiss. And then . . .

But once again this is hard to explain. You see, it's really difficult now to say who exactly did the kissing — I mean, whose tongue it was that poked forward and searched the inside of a mouth. Not gentle and soft either. Really thrusting and aggressive. Whose? All I know for sure is that it happened and that we pulled away and stared at each other.

I must say, she seemed surprised enough. But then that was the way I felt too. In fact for a moment there the whole experience really threw me. I felt as though somebody had stood me on my head, because all at once the whole world felt upside down. I didn't know where I was. I honestly don't think I'd have been surprised if Anna had suddenly slipped a note into my hand — something like, "Only two weeks to go. Save it up for me. See you then, lover." At least I'd have known where I was.

But as usual nothing happened. And the next minute Ken and Anna are getting ready to leave on their honeymoon and all the guests are pushing past me. Until finally I'm left there on my own in the middle of the lawn. That was when the old man, the Quaker who'd made the speech in the hall, came up.

"A beautiful couple," he says, beaming all over his face. "A fine young man and a remarkable young woman."

As he spoke, I glanced over towards the car. Anna was just about to slide into the front seat. But right at the last she hesitated and peered at the crowd as though searching for someone. Evidently it was me she was after, because the moment she spots me in the background she stands on tip-toe and quickly blows me a kiss. And for the life of me I couldn't read it. A gentle farewell kiss? A sisterly kiss? A promise of things to come? A fuck you jack I'm all right kiss? God knows. And if He doesn't let on, who am I to say. So that's the way it is, I think. And no sooner has the thought flashed through my head than — Bang! All that floating feeling, all that purity crap, is shot to hell. And with a thump I'm down on the solid ground again, with everything back to normal.

I can't say it was a great sensation. And yet funnily enough it wasn't too bad either. In some ways almost better than that floaty, pure stuff. A kind of relief. The old solid world back again. Welcome home, I say to myself, and I pick up a full glass of champagne from the table next to me. Before I can drink it though, the old man puts his arm across my shoulder in a brotherly sort of way — and as he does so, I hear the car door bang closed.

"Yes," he says again, somehow sad and happy together, "a remarkable young woman."

By then the glass is almost to my lips — I can see his face distorted through the curve of the rim. And I pause just long enough to say:

"Amen, brother, amen."

# Hobbies

I wouldn't say I was lonely after Di left. For one thing, I knew she'd be back. There was nowhere in particular for her to go, and she'd had no real reason for leaving in the first place. All she'd said the day she walked out was, The trouble with you is you don't know you're alive. And what kind of reason is that? No, it was a foregone conclusion, her coming back, and the only thing I had to do was sit around and wait, just bide my time.

That was easy enough during the week, when I was working, but it did get a bit tedious at weekends. Early on, I decided that what I needed was a hobby, something to take me out of myself; and as I'm not one to let ideas go cold, I was soon trying out a few possibilities. Fishing, for instance. But sitting on a river bank all day with nothing to do except mull over the past wasn't exactly my style. Nor was photography. There's something unsettling about it, the way little portions of the world you don't normally notice suddenly leap out at you once you train a lens on them. So I gave that up too. Then I hit on the idea of fossicking, hunting for semi-precious stones and such like. It was about the time I heard Di had shacked up with a bloke in Sydney. That won't last, I thought, and I bought myself a shovel, a sieve, and a few other odds and ends, and set off.

As things turned out, it was just what I needed, exactly the right mixture of activity and interest. Shovelling away at an old slag heap or sandy river bed, you don't have a lot of time to dwell on your own troubles. Also, living fairly close to the New England area as I do, there was no shortage of streams and abandoned mines to get stuck in to. Anyway, before long I was exploring all over the region, and what had started out as a hobby pretty soon became a whole lot more. Within a month or two I could hardly wait for Fridays to come round, and during the week I spent more and more time in the public library reading up on geology and the collecting and cutting of stones. I don't mind admitting that there were whole long periods during the subsequent two years when I hardly gave Di a thought.

The amazing thing was the way I got d[...] not as though I was particularly lucky. True[...] odd piece of topaz and coloured agate, eve[...] ments of sapphire. But that's all. No[...] spectacular. Not until I discovered the gul[...] the gully was a different story altogether.

I stumbled on it the day after I received[...] Someone I'd regarded as a mutual friend ra[...] Thursday night and told me she was genuin[...] the bloke in Sydney, that as far as she w[...] this was it. Naturally I didn't take much[...] never been one to believe in idle gossip — n[...] true and lasting love come to that. Not i[...] Though I was a bit angry at being dished up[...] second hand. It made me feel out of sort[...] and I decided the next day to take a sickie.

I suppose that's how I came to discov[...] Usually, before I set out on a trip, I had a[...] the map and decided exactly where I w[...] that Friday morning I just chucked a few t[...] car and drove off without really deciding a[...] knows where I went to. The only thing that sticks in my mind is climbing up onto the ridge in the late afternoon and finding myself unexpectedly looking down into the gully. At one time it must have been part of a water course. But then, as now, it was bone dry: a deep, badly eroded cleft, arid and sandy at the bottom, stretching away for a mile or two — with just one small pool at the near end, fed by a trickle of water that oozes out of the steep hillside. It's an uncanny sort of place, cut off from the surrounding country: almost invisible until you're right above it; and once you're down at the bottom, like a world apart, with tall bare hillsides on either hand, pretty hot most of the time, and with hardly anything growing in it below the few straggly gum trees that line the tops of the slopes. Not exactly a pretty place, though private enough. And also, given my interests, possessing one distinct advantage: the sandy floor is rich with fragments of precious and semi-precious stones: hard splinters of yellow and blue sapphire; whole crystals of clear brown topaz; translucent pebbles or curves of red and grey agate; even tiny chips of diamond if your luck's in.

I began collecting that very afternoon; and when I arrived home, I put what I'd found in a separate box, a whole new collection. It was like a special store, a proof of what I'd been doing while she was away squandering her life. A kind of account. I remember thinking, wait until she sees these; let her measure all the wasted months against this.

I went to the gully every weekend after that. Once, she wrote and asked for a divorce. But I ignored the letter — and the frantic phone calls as well, that she made soon afterwards. I knew she would eventually come to her senses. In any case, I was too busy cutting and mounting stones, or working out there on the hot sand, shovelling and sieving for all I was worth. It was damned hard work, and without water to help, I had to spit on any likely stones and then hold them up to the sun, to see what I'd found. Always, in the evenings, when I put the day's collection together, it smelt of dried spittle — the way my mother's handkerchief smelt when I was a boy, when she licked the cloth and wiped smudges of tears off my cheeks. Of course, I washed each stone thoroughly, made it clean, before storing it for cutting. The beauty of sapphires, especially, with their hard clear colouring, is always contaminated somehow by too much human contact.

I soon had quite a heap of real finds. Mind you, don't get me wrong, I didn't just kick the stones out of the sand: every one of them was the result of hours of digging. Yet I did enjoy the work: the sheer mindless strain of shifting hundredweights of sand; and every time I straightened up, seeing nothing but the barren glare of the valley. All on my own there, with no one to bother or question me, protected by the tall dry walls of the hillsides. Almost like a fragment of animated stone myself, encased in all that sand. Completely private, where even her fruitless phone calls couldn't reach.

Actually that's not completely true. About the privacy, I mean. Because as it turned out I wasn't the only one who knew about the gully. There was also Sol, and his wife Ruby. Though in one sense they don't count, because they went there for a different purpose altogether.

The first Saturday I came across them really gave me a turn. I'd parked the car and slithered down the slope towards the small water hole, because that was the easiest place to get down. And there they were. You'd have thought it was Bondi Beach to look at them: Sol sitting perched on an aluminium deck chair under a striped umbrella; their kid playing with a bucket in the sand; and Ruby hovering around with that nervous, infuriating air of hers.

"Have a jar," Sol said, before I could even introduce myself, and he pointed towards the water hole.

I didn't answer for a minute and I must have looked a

right loon standing there gaping. It wasn't just the unexpectedness of finding them: it was Sol himself, the look of the bloke. He wasn't like anybody you've ever seen before, which makes him a bit difficult to describe. At a rough guess I'd say he was about six foot six and built with it. A bloody giant in fact. With a great gut on him, hands like crane scoops, and a big round face nearly as red as Ayers Rock — or so I thought at that stage; because I hadn't yet seen him at the end of the day. His kid, I should mention, was a sort of miniature replica. While Ruby was quite the opposite: a little stick of a thing, always buzzing round him and worrying about him, as nervous as hell.

Anyway, there I was suddenly facing them all.

"Go on," he said, "help yourself."

I looked into the shallow pool, and at the bottom, in a wicker basket, there must have been at least three dozen quarts of beer.

"It's a bit early for me," I stammered out. Which was true: it was barely eight o'clock. "Maybe later when I've worked up a thirst."

"Suit yourself," Sol said. "But don't blame me if there's none left when you come back."

I didn't quite understand.

"You mean you're expecting company?" I asked gloomily, thinking how the gully would be overrun with people.

That was when Ruby stepped in.

"Oh no," she said, sort of proud and sad at the same time, "they're all for Sol."

"All?" I said, and had another quick look at the heap of bottles.

"Yes," she added. "It's his hobby, drinking beer. We can't afford it too often. Only once a week or so. Then we usually come here, where it's quiet, and he can enjoy himself."

Well you can imagine, I thought I'd stumbled on a right couple of nuts; and I excused myself as best I could and left them to it.

I didn't feel too great though. I expected them to start pestering me, asking me a lot of questions. But not on your life: I didn't see or hear them the whole day. The gully might just as well have been deserted for all the noise they made.

They were starting to pack up when I finally threw it in, late in the afternoon, and made my way back to the path above the water hole. The first thing I noticed was the wicker basket sitting empty on the sand; and straight afterwards, Sol standing there with a skinful. Not swaying or anything: just standing stock still, holding himself rock steady, his face really red now — his head like the top of one of those old-fashioned post boxes.

"How's it going?" I asked — not because I was particularly interested: it was more a way of getting past them without appearing rude.

Ruby smiled thinly, her face worried now more than sad; but still as nervous and fussy as ever. She didn't ask me any questions; they never did poke their noses into my business.

I started to clamber up the path, and that was when Sol spoke.

"It's what a man needs," he said, "a hobby. Something to look forward to; to remind him he's still alive."

His voice was a bit on the thickish side, but not particularly drunk.

"You're right there," I said. "There's nothing like a hobby to keep you in touch."

Well, what else could I have answered? And I cleared out as quickly as I could.

From then on I got used to seeing them there. God knows why he chose a spot like that to do his drinking in. But they didn't bother me any, so who was I to care. I appreciated that, the way they didn't snoop. They never so much as asked me what I'd found in the course of the day. Not once. And I certainly wasn't keen to volunteer that kind of information without a lot of prompting.

Except for that one occasion, of course: I nearly blurted it all out then. It was the day Di came back; or rather the afternoon before her return — she arrived in the early evening, just before I reached home. It's funny how everything came together.

Naturally I wasn't to know she was on her way back, though I'd never doubted it was going to happen sometime or other. I'd gone out in the morning as usual, said hello to Sol and Ruby who were there ahead of me, and immediately got stuck into digging down to a slab of rock I'd located the week before. For most of the day everything went normally: I suppose I had about average luck, which in the gully means I did pretty well. By fairly late in the afternoon I'd cleared almost right along the rock shelf. There were only a couple of square yards of sand left and I very nearly decided to give those away. It's a bloody good job I didn't, because it was during that last half hour that I struck it rich, as they used to say. I couldn't believe it at first: this great big pebble sitting there in the sieve, sort of bluey-white and faintly soapy to touch. But it was a diamond all right: there was no room for doubt once I'd held it up to the light. And close to being flawless; just a couple of slight fractures along one edge.

I think my first reaction was simply to sit down on the sand. With the diamond clutched in my hand, the whole gully looked more beautiful than ever: totally closed in on itself; perfect; nothing moving or growing anywhere; with the last yellow rays of the sun turning the upper slopes into a series of dark, purplish folds.

About as close as you could get on earth to a clear lunar landscape.

For a while there, I actually felt as though I'd been a bit touched by the moon. I was that excited. Suddenly, all I wanted to do was blurt it out, tell somebody, and I collected my gear together and hurried over to see if Sol and his missus were still there.

As it happened, they'd just packed up and Ruby was trying to get Sol up the bank.

"Did you have a good day?" I asked, hoping they'd return the compliment and give me a chance to tell them my news.

But I got no response. Sol was so bloody tight he could hardly stand up and his face looked as though it was about to explode.

"Help me," Ruby said, her voice really desperate, as though it was the end of the world or something. So I put down my gear and between us we coaxed and pushed Sol up to the top.

He didn't help us any. Every few paces or so he'd stop and hold forth about his stupid bloody hobby — as though drinking could ever be graced by that title.

"There's nothing like a hobby," he kept saying. "It keeps you on the straight and narrow, helps you remember what living's all about. Worth more than all the other shit put together."

I didn't argue with him: I was too busy pushing his great fat behind. We got him up eventually and went back and collected the baby and all the other stuff.

"Thank you so much," Ruby said, genuinely grateful.

But I wasn't interested in her gratitude: all I could think of was the diamond that was damn near burning a hole in my pocket.

"Look," I said, "don't thank me. Why not meet me at the local pub and have a beer with me. That'd be nearer the mark."

She started to shake her head, but Sol had heard me as well.

"Bloody right," he said. "Now you're talking."

I could see Ruby didn't like it, but she agreed and climbed into the car. I didn't wait around for them though: I was too full of the joys to drive slowly. And by the time I reached the pub I was some way ahead of them. Not that it mattered: it was my shout, so I got the beers all ready — two for Sol, because it seemed a bit of a cheek getting only one glassful for a man like that.

They arrived a few minutes later. He plonked himself down in the chair, his great fat gut pressing against the table, and in two shakes he'd downed both the beers. But even he had his limits, and that very nearly finished him. He hiccuped a few times, swayed dangerously to one side, and almost fell over onto the floor.

"Sol!" Ruby cried out, her voice all panicky.

"It's awright," he said thickly.

And slowly he stood up and walked ponderously over to the gents. His face wasn't red any more: it was a sort of blotchy, mauvy colour.

"Well . . ." I said, once he was gone, intending to start telling her about the stone I'd found.

But I never got the chance.

"He's killing himself," she said, her face somehow pulled out of shape by the lines of worry.

I'd never seen her look quite so thin and frail and anxious before.

"Oh, I wouldn't say that," I murmured.

"Can't you see?" she broke out. "Are you blind or something?" — which I thought was a bit strong. "Him and his damned hobby! Aren't there other things in life apart from that? There's his family, his son, to think of too!" She hugged the little red-faced baby to herself as though it was Sol in person. "I don't want to stop him drinking altogether. If he'd only cut it down, think of our feelings sometimes."

There was a lot more like that — I can't remember it all. Some of it I found a bit hard to take.

"It is his own life, after all," I said at one point.

"No, not just his," she burst out. "Mine as well. What would I ever do without him?"

Which is always my cue for getting out. I drained my glass, excused myself, and headed for home. And there was Di, after more than two years away, waiting for me.

"Glad to see you," I said, and took out the plastic jar in which I put all my best finds of the day and placed it on the table between us.

"He didn't want me," she said quietly.

"Who? The bloke in Sydney?"

"Yes. He just threw me out."

"Look," I said quickly, "I don't wish to know anything about that. As far as I'm concerned, this is your home. This is where you belong, and if you want to come back there's a place here for you."

"Just like that?" she asked disbelieving.

"Just like that," I affirmed.

"But where do we start after all this?"

"We start right here," I said, and I opened the jar, took out the big bluish diamond, and placed it in front of her

"No, really," she said, pushing it aside. "I'm being serious."

I'd been sidetracked enough for one day, however: I wasn't having any more of it.

"So am I," I said, and I put the big smooth stone right into her hand. "That's a diamond," I said, "the biggest uncut diamond you'll ever see. Look at it. Hold it up to the light. Millions of years were needed to make that; and locked up inside there is the perfect stone. Perfect."

She looked at it for a while: even held it up to the light. But only for a few seconds — she wasn't really interested. Then she let her hand fall back on to the table and she started to cry.

"He didn't want me," she said unhappily. "He told me he didn't care what I did with my life as long as I cleared out."

I should perhaps say at this point that Di is a tall well-built woman. She can on occasion look quite brilliant. But there was nothing very brilliant about her right then. She seemed to be smaller than usual, almost shrivelled. In some ways, seeing her like that, I was reminded of Ruby's thin anxious face, the woman in her pared away by things she couldn't ever hope to control. And for a moment I came close to appreciating Sol's point of view, to understanding why it was he drank.

"Never mind," I said. "You've done the right thing."

And I took the stone from her hand and put it away safely.

"Is that all you can say?" she almost shouted.

But I wasn't arguing with her, not on that of all days.

"You'll feel better about it in the morning," I said, and I walked through to the bedroom.

We've never really discussed the matter since. Di is still with me — I don't know for how long. If she had the chance, she might leave again; but then she might not. It's hard to say. In any case, she'd probably come back. Life rarely gives you what you think you deserve — least of all what you desire. As for me, I expect very little. I've now had the diamond cut and I keep it in a private box in the bank. Every week or so, I go and look at it and hold it: the hard faceted feel of the cold stone; glowing with its own blue-white light. The nearest thing in this life to eternity. Millions of years in the growing, born of the lower, subterranean fires that no human being has ever witnessed and survived. As close as we'll ever get to the indestructible. It took me a long time, and some pain, to discover that. Pacing empty rooms and waiting with a certitude which might never find any echo from without — out there in the uncertain world. I remember those days sometimes. But they all slip away, dissolve, whenever I stand alone in the vault, the blue-white rose of stone resting in the palm of my hand. Unchanged.

Di has come with me once or twice. She cups her hand under that precious pool of light, looks at it askance — half-fascinated, half-repelled; taking refuge in feigned indifference. It's the same with my trips to the gully. Perhaps once a month, sometimes less, she accompanies me. I've never known her to search for more than half an hour at a stretch. Most of the time she sits on the sand gazing up at the dry slopes as though they're some kind of barrier to her secret desires. I work on, saying very little, thinking occasionally of Sol who hasn't appeared in the gully again. Obviously he must have found some kind of answer. Personally, as I say, I don't expect too much — I certainly don't expect to find another such perfect stone. I know full well that only ever happens once — and only then if you're lucky.

Whenever Di appears particularly down, I say to her: "Give me a hand. It'll take your mind off things."

But she shakes her head and stretches back on the dry, absorbent sand, gazing up at the clear opal of the sky. That's always been her trouble: she's never managed to learn much from experience. You might say that what she needs is a hobby.

# Secret Life

The first time he went there it was exactly what he was looking for: long stretches of beach with not a soul to disturb him. Walking four or five miles each morning, over the dry sand or on the edge of the sea, as far as the lagoon. A perfect oval of blue water fringed with bush, where he could sit in the silence of the surf and imagine the secret life in the warm shallows. Stirring down there between the fronds of glistening weed. Schools of brightly coloured fish darting through the greenish sunlight; smooth-skinned, harmless snakes breasting the surface and crawling out onto the hard-packed sand when there was nobody there to perceive them. Undisturbed. Basking in the warm sun and spray.

He thought it would be like that again when he went back the following year. He rose early on the first morning and set out. Already beginning to think of the beach as his own. Stripping off his T-shirt and trunks as soon as he was clear of the small cluster of cottages. But when he had gone less than a mile, he saw someone else on the beach, in the distance, walking towards him. As they came closer, he could make out that it was a woman; a few moments later, that she too was young and nude. He hesitated a while, and then stopped to slip on his trunks — noticing almost simultaneously that she was also putting her costume back on.

They passed within forty yards of each other: she, further down, splashing through the fringes of the surf; he, following the high-tide mark. They neither of them waved nor gave any sign. But at a reasonable distance, they again stopped and stripped off their clothes.

As he stepped out of his trunks, he found that he was blushing slightly, feeling ridiculous at the absurdity of their ritual. And although he saw nobody else afterwards, that small incident changed the tone of the day. Even the lagoon wasn't quite so secret and undisturbed as he remembered it — his eyes constantly being drawn to the clear arc of footprints which traced its shoreline.

He passed her every morning after that. Always with the same pantomime of donning and discarding clothes. It was a set pattern now which neither of them could break. The only difference was that he found himself nodding to her — a sign which by the fifth morning had grown into a wave of recognition. Also, by then, it was no longer the lagoon which captured his imagination. He still sat beside it, but thinking now mainly of the girl. Imagining her fair hair, silky and fine; her skin, clear and brown, so smooth that it was almost without texture, smelling only of the sea through which she splashed each morning.

It was on that fifth day, in the evening, that he drove into Nambucca, for a meal. The restaurant on the busy highway, shaken by the occasional semi-trailer that thundered past. He had barely begun eating when she came over to his table and introduced herself. But he recognized her even before she spoke.

"Please, won't you join me?" he said, hearing in his own voice the same formality which governed their daily ritual on the beach.

She, too, was stiff and formal to begin with. But after the meal she began to relax.

"Are you here on holiday?" he asked her.

"Yes," she said, "I'm up from Sydney. I love it here, it's so peaceful and secluded. A million miles from buses and crowds — and work!" Laughing at her own attitudes. "Escaping from reality I suppose. All that clean air and space, it's not real." Laughing again. "My secret life on the North Coast."

"Do you believe in secret lives?" he said, smiling back at her.

But he wasn't really joining in the conversation. While she spoke, he noticed that her hair wasn't fine as he had imagined, but thick and bushy, almost wiry. The word coarse crossed his mind, and he dismissed it quickly. Shifting his attention to her hands which fidgeted nervously, to the way she picked at her nails that were bitten down. Thin, ordinary fingers, almost pathetic in a way.

And yet he had to admit she was attractive. Different from what he had expected, but at the same time desirable. That thought kept coming back to him, in spite of his vague disappointment, and when it was time to leave, he said:

"Would you like to come to my house for a drink?"

She hesitated, but not because of shyness as he at first supposed.

"Or my place if you like," she said. "I'd love you to see my cottage. Hidden away in the bush. It's like a dream. Not a real house at all."

He followed the dust coils of her car along the track, the headlights burrowing into the darkness of night and bush, discovering her hidden cottage. He saw at once that there was nothing dream-like about it. Just an ordinary wooden house. Probably a kit-home, carted to the site in prefabricated sections.

But he went inside without a word, caught up now by the familiar sequence of events. The drink, the idle conversation, sitting close beside her on the couch, gauging the moment for that first critical move. Both exciting and at the same time uneventful. Somehow known in advance. Each move practised and repeated on at least a dozen other occasions.

The only thing which surprised him was something she said later. They were lying in bed together, listening to the distant surf, almost on the verge of sleep.

"It's just as if I was someone else," she murmured, "not me at all. Some other person that I hardly know. Hiding away here with you. Like being on another planet which nobody else knows about."

He slept soon afterwards, an unusually dreamless sleep. And when he awoke in the greyish morning light she was lying on the far side of the bed, curled up and alone, her back turned towards him. He saw for the first time that her skin was not really smooth at all, not as he had pictured it. Across her shoulders there was a fine down of fair hair, the skin itself starred with tiny interconnected pores; while in the small of her back a brown patch showed clearly, probably a birth mark, oval shaped and brushed with a trace of dark fur. Secret and faintly animal in its suggestion.

His initial impulse was to steal quietly away, to leave the house without her knowing. But already she was stirring, turning towards him. Kissing his chest and the underside of his chin.

"Ugh, bristles!" she said, laughing, "take them away!"

But snuggling closer.

He also laughed, rasping his chin against her thick hair, but taking care not to let his hands slide down her back, to where he had seen the brown blemish of the birthmark. Having to will himself to respond to her now. Slightly unnerved by her moans and cries as she abandoned herself to the lonely intimacy of this place she had brought him to.

Later, after they had showered and eaten, she suggested that they go for a walk on the beach.

"Without having to do any quick change acts," she said, laughing.

Always laughing, it seemed to him. Parading before him in the nude, the dark oval blemish almost hidden by the curve of her back. But still visible if he looked.

"No, I can't go this morning," he said quickly. "I have to drive in to Coffs Harbour. Only for an hour."

"Can't you put it off?" she asked, disappointed. He shook his head.

"Then I'll wait here for you to come back," she said.

"No," he replied hastily, "you go for a walk anyway. Wait for me by the lagoon. I'll be able to meet you there by mid-morning."

From the front window of his own cottage, overlooking the sea, he saw her walking slowly up the beach. A single, isolated figure. Difficult to imagine now.

Before she moved out of sight, his suitcase was packed and the cottage locked; and by the time she reached the lagoon, he had driven through Coffs Harbour, following the Pacific Highway north.

He stopped near where the road turned inland. At Red Rock. Hiring a small run-down cottage fronting onto the estuary.

In the afternoon he walked through to the deserted beach, alone once again. Plodding along the hard gritty sand to the end of the bay and climbing up onto the headland. From the top, he could see a school of dolphins lazily feeding just beyond the line of the surf. Their bodies breaking the surface on the slope of the swell. Their skins silver-grey against the greenish tone of the sea, unnaturally smooth, unblemished, occasionally catching and reflecting the blue tint of the sky.

Watching them move slowly backwards and forwards across the wide mouth of the bay, diving and surfacing at regular intervals, he found it easy to imagine their secret life down there in the depths. Beyond his vision. The smooth silent bodies touching each other in the darkness; undulating between perfect sea-bed gardens of rock and waving weed; the silver or rainbow flash of tiny fish, transfiguring the stillness; the slow upward spiral towards the blue dome of light. A perfect dance of silence. Hidden from any prying eyes.

With a sigh, he stood up. A true experience, he thought contentedly, as he turned back towards the land.

# Three Faces of Terry Couzens

## I

Terry was bad enough when he was working. Always the armchair revolutionary, a regular Che Guevara of the suburbs. But after he gave up the boutique he got even worse. Living out his theories, he called it. Perched up there on the tablelands in Northern New South Wales. In a derelict old cocky's cottage on a scrap of land wedged between farms. "I've dropped out," he said in the letter. But who ever heard of a forty-seven year old dropout? I should have saved myself the trip up, ignored those romantic appeals of his. "It'll be like old times," he wrote. "Trips up the North Coast; days spent in the bush; all-night parties." He made it sound so bloody simple and carefree, and as usual I fell for it.

I arrived late in the afternoon of New Year's Eve and I was no sooner out of the van than he was down off the verandah and all over me. As though I was his long lost brother.

"My Christ it's great to see you!"

Bellowing it out to the whole hillside. Hugging me and slapping me on the back for all he was worth. Always the great one for enthusiasm, our Terry.

"Glad to see you, Terry," I said weakly.

Though to tell the truth I hardly recognized him. Big as ever and still with a droopy gut, but now with hair all over the place. Long pepper-and-salt beard; wild looking grey curls hanging round his shoulders; even growing extra on his chest — great gingery-grey tufts of it pushing over the top of his grubby singlet. And with plenty of body odour to match.

"Great things have happened since I left the Smoke," he said expansively. "Let me show you round."

Not even giving me time to get a toothbrush out of the van. Dragging me straight off on the grand tour. A whole bloody hour spent walking round that crummy seven acres of dirt inspecting his unfinished projects. The same wherever you looked. The garden planned and staked out, but not dug or planted. ("Self-supporting by next year," he assured me.) Some scraps of tooled leather hanging from the shed rafters. Bits and pieces of loom stacked against the wall and a great pile of raw wool mouldering in the corner. ("Every bit of it plucked," I was told solemnly. "None of your shearing here. Ruins the staple.") The same with the pottery: two rusty tubs of mud dug from the hillside. ("You've got to start from basics.")

And so it went on. You could see at a glance it was nothing but a shambles. But not to Terry.

"This is the life," he said, looking proudly out over the six foot high thickets of blackberry and a few sad-looking gums festooned with mistletoe. "Back to the authentic experience. None of your city living any more."

That was a dig at me.

"You should chuck it all in as well," he went on. "Clear out of Sydney and come up here."

A brotherly arm around my shoulder and an extra dose of the body odour.

"Not Sydney, Terry," I corrected him, "Newcastle."

But he wasn't listening.

"A bloke can really feel free in a place like this. Nobody on your back. No social conventions to get in the way. Every day a new beginning. And you make the rules. No other bugger to tell you to do this or that. An island of freedom and peace right in the middle of all this ratshit called society."

"Aren't you exaggerating a bit, Terry?" I said doubtfully, looking at the buckled iron on the roof and the sagging weather board, unpainted, cracked and splitting at the corners.

"Not on your life, mate. You see that lot out there?" One dirty fingernail pointing vaguely in the direction of the nearest hilltops. "When you're a kid, you're told it's run on a principle called the division of labour. Well I've got a better word for it. I call it debt. Everybody's in debt to someone else. There's no community any more. You don't rely on other people. You just owe them something. Every bugger in debt to someone else. One bloody great money transaction."

"And you reckon you've beaten the system?"

"My word! See for yourself" — which as an argument didn't exactly knock me out.

"Hang on, Terry," I objected. "You can't cut yourself off completely. What about money? Surely you can't do without it altogether."

"Money!" he said contemptuously. "Did you say money!" And then a crafty look suddenly coming into his eyes. "I'll show you what I think of dollars and cents."

Laughing now, he hauled me off to the kitchen. The usual chaos. Piles of dirty dishes everywhere; scraps of food on the floor; grease stains all over the walls. I thought for a minute I'd been taken there to see all the mess. Another of his achievements. But kicking aside a couple of old cooking pots, he opened a cupboard.

"Feast your eyes on that lot," he said, and pointed to three shelves stacked with full bottles of whisky. "Every cent I own invested there."

I must admit I'm partial to a drop of whisky, so I didn't say a thing.

"That's the only wealth I'm interested in. Pure liquid gold." Holding one bottle up to the window so the late afternoon sunlight shone through it. "The sort of wealth that gives pleasure. That you can share with your friends."

On that score, at least, he was as good as his word, because soon after dark the cars started arriving for the New Year's Eve party. All his old friends — that's what he called them anyway. To me they looked the usual bunch of hangers-on he'd always knocked around with.

Not that it mattered to me how he wanted to waste his whisky. A party is a party as far as I'm concerned. I'll drink with the devil himself if he pays. And this was no exception. I might even have enjoyed myself given a fair go. But as usual Terry stuffed it up.

For one thing he was half-pissed by ten o'clock. And what's worse, he was in one of his noisy reckless moods. Charging all over the house, shouting and laughing, and generally making a public nuisance of himself. In particular, I noticed how he had his eye on this woman, forever putting his arm round her or giving her a quick feel. She was a bit past it if you ask me and her little fat boy friend was getting as shat off as hell. His belly and chin would start to tremble with anger every time Terry went near her.

But once Terry had got that dead-set look in his bleary eyes, there was no stopping him. And I guessed he'd be humping her before the night was very much older. What just about bowled me over, though, was where he made his attempt. Right there in the kitchen! The two of them wedged in the corner behind the old fridge. It was asking for trouble. And sure enough the little fat boy friend went snooping out there and caught them at it.

"You bastard!" he shouted. "Why can't you get your own woman?"

And he gave Terry a crack across the ear. Which, considering his size, was a bloody stupid thing to do.

Because without even bothering to do up his fly, Terry pulled free and belted him one — and down the little bloke went. Then, as if that wasn't insult enough, Terry had to go and read him a lecture.

"She's not your woman or mine," he said. "You'd better get that into your little skull right now. There's no private ownership in this house. Everything's communal property."

All that in a drunken voice, while he stood there with his wang dangling free, only a few feet from the poor bugger's face.

Well, understandably, the little bloke was livid. He couldn't have another go at Terry — he just wasn't big enough. So he did the next best thing. He jumped up, grabbed a full bottle of whisky from the open cupboard, and chucked it straight at Terry's head.

Fortunately, he wasn't much of a shot — it bounced off the wall and smashed harmlessly on the floor. But now it was Terry's turn to be angry.

"My bloody whisky!" he roared out.

Lunging forward, he grabbed the little bloke by the shirt. He wasn't going to stick around and get punched again though. With one terrified jerk, he tore himself right out of the shirt, and with his little fat tits wobbling in the breeze he went running through the house, Terry close behind him.

I'll give him his due, the little bloke, despite his short legs he could really run. Going like the clappers he was. Off the verandah, down the overgrown driveway, and across the road towards the paddock. Pulling ahead of Terry at every stride, his bare sweaty skin all shiny in the moonlight. And he would have got clean away. Except that what he didn't realize was that there was an electric fence all along the grass verge.

The next thing there was this blue flash, a kind of crack, and up he went into the air. Just as if some invisible foot had booted him straight up the arse. It was like being hit by Terry again, only much worse. With an effort, he managed to get up, and left to himself he would probably have been all right. But Terry had to have the last word.

"Get off, you capitalist bastard!" he yelled out.

At the sound of that voice he panicked and charged into the fence again. Performance repeated, of course. Though this time he really looked bloody groggy. Luckily, he'd landed on the far side of the wire. Even so, it was all he could do to stumble off across the paddock.

Great hilarity after that. Everyone laughing and describing what they'd seen. But it didn't last. Once the general excitement had died down, the whole episode somehow put a damper on proceedings. Especially where Terry was concerned. He turned so morose I don't think he even finished that screw in the corner. Just withdrew to his bedroom with a bottle and left the party to fizzle out. Some New Year! No Auld Lang Syne — no goodwill to all men — no nothing.

And as if that wasn't bad enough, we were woken up first thing next morning by the little fat bloke's woman, her face all tear-stained and worried.

"I can't find him," she wailed. "I waited down at the house and he never turned up."

Well, you can imagine — panic stations! Terry, looking like death after his night on the booze, lumbering down the driveway to spearhead the search.

Not that it took us long. We found him at the bottom of the hill, lying in a dammed-up puddle of dirty water in the bed of the creek. As peaceful as you please. So much so, that I thought he was a goner for a minute. But in fact he was still breathing and we got him straight off to a doctor.

It turned out that he'd had a heart seizure. And what

with that, and lying out there in the open the whole night — not even a shirt to cover him, exposed to all the cold and dew — he was really in a bad way. But as always Terry's luck held. After an anxious hour at the hospital it became clear that the bloke was going to pull through.

Still, it didn't exactly get the New Year off to a bright start, and the rest of the day was positively dismal. Terry just sat around on the verandah glooming for all he was worth.

Now if there's one thing I can't stand, it's guilt and regret over things past and done with. There's no point in it. So I was soon pissed off with the heavy silence.

"A fine bloody holiday this is turning out to be," I said.

No answer. Terry slumped there in the chair moodily scratching his gut through a hole in his singlet.

"Listen," I said to him at last, "nobody's to blame. It's one of those things that happen, that's all."

"Is that what you really think?" he said, and I wasn't sure if he was being sarcastic or not.

"All right," I said, trying a different tack, "have it your own way. You're as guilty as hell, solely to blame. Does that make you feel better?"

Again no answer. Scratching an armpit now.

"Oh for Christ's sake snap out of it, Terry!" I said impatiently. "Go and have a whisky or something. Drink some of that communal wealth you're hoarding in the kitchen."

He brightened up a bit when I suggested that. He sat there thoughtful for a minute or two, then went through to the back. And I assumed he'd taken my advice.

But not a chance. I was just beginning to wonder what was keeping him when I heard this crash and the sound of breaking glass. I tell you, it really gave me a shock. I thought — he's cutting his wrists — and I was out of that chair and through the house like a shot.

I found him out at the back. No slashed wrists or throat. No tears of grief. Just standing there with a big cardboard box filled with what remained of the whisky. And he was taking the bottles one by one and throwing them against the old brick chimney.

"What the fuck are you doing?" I shouted.

Another bottle whizzed through the air and exploded in a shower of drops and glass.

"That's bloody good whisky you're wasting there!" I protested.

Two more bottles in quick succession, one of them missing the chimney and smashing on the roof. Faint sounds of whisky gurgling in the gutter.

"Oh come on, Terry! What are you trying to prove?"

The next bottle narrowly missed me and crashed through the kitchen window. Quick as I could, I was inside with the door firmly closed. If he wanted to act like a fool, that was his business. Never get between a man and his guilt, that's my motto.

I must say, though, it did seem to do him good, all that stupid destruction. He definitely looked better when he came back in. Sort of relieved. In fact he seemed so much more relaxed that I even ventured to have a go at him.

"That was a great display, that was," I said sarcastically. "You really achieved a lot out there. D'you know that? A great step forward for the revolutionary cause."

"Bugger off!" he growled.

"No, really," I insisted. "You really proved your independence there. Showed your total contempt for the economy of waste."

But sarcasm was always wasted on Terry.

"You can say what you please," he said, with an

attempt at what I suppose he regarded as dignity. "But personally I believe in paying my debts."

## II

There was a time when Terry would fish right round the clock given the opportunity. Mad for it he was. Sea or river, it made no difference. Perched dangerously on some wave-soaked rock or up to his chin in muddy water — it was all the same just as long as there were fish about. Great days. The two of us out there on our own, miles from anywhere, exploring the depths with long raking casts. I tell you, no self-respecting fish had a hope when we were in form. So naturally, after we'd recovered from that lousy party, I suggested an afternoon with the rods.

But to my amazement he turned it down flat.

"I've given it up," he said.

I could hardly believe my ears.

"Go on," I said, thinking he was pulling my leg. "With all these rivers here on the tablelands? Right here on your doorstop?"

But he meant it all right. I could tell by the way he stood there scratching his crotch, all thoughtful and serious.

"I've become a vegetarian," he said. "I don't side with blood sports any more."

"Blood sports! You call fishing a blood sport! For Christ's sake, the rivers and dams are full of fish. What's the point of them being there if we don't catch them?"

"That's typical of you these days," he said, really withering. "A creature of appetites. You've got no respect for the sanctity of life."

"And since when have you had that kind of respect?"

"Since I had a good look at the fuck-up that calls

itself society and saw how much aggression there is in it." Hitching up his old jeans and sucking in his belly so he could get the waistband over the bulge — smartening himself up before delivering the big lecture. "Ever since he climbed out of the trees, man's been busy raping this planet. A born killer. If it moves, bash it one — that's the lesson of history. Well a few of us have had enough. Everything has a right to life. The freedom to do its own thing without fear of being zapped between the eyes by some aggressive bastard."

"And what do you expect me to do about it?" I said, on the defensive now. "Chuck my rods away?"

"You can suit yourself," he said, being consistent for once. "We're both free to do as we please."

So in the end that was how we worked it out. Off to the Gwydir in the van; and while I fished in the deep pools, Terry mucked around in the shallows panning for gold and looking for semi-precious stones.

But somehow it wasn't the same. No mutual interest, I suppose. Personally, I couldn't get worked up about a few tiny specks of gold or a lump of coloured rock. And as for Terry — on the one occasion when I yelled out that I'd had a bite, he didn't so much as twitch a buttock.

It really got to me eventually. Seeing him so bloody absorbed. Scrabbling around there in the sand and gravel.

"You know what your trouble is, Terry?" I called out. "You're a frustrated capitalist."

That got him going. He was straight up out of the river, water dripping from his beard and running down between the gravy stains on his singlet. Like some wild old man of the bush.

"You'd better wash your mouth out!" he said angrily.

"Well, look at you," I said. "Grovelling there for a bit of gold. The old profit motive's got you by the balls."

"That's all you know about it," he answered, scornful as hell. "This is a way of life, not a search for profit. You just can't bear seeing someone do something creative."

"Creative! What's creative about that?"

"I'll tell you Mr Clever-prick. Because when I've got enough of this dust, I'm going to make it into a ring. A perfect form. Something that'll last umpteen lifetimes — a thing of beauty."

I was about to tell him he could do with some beautifying himself. But I didn't get a chance because at that moment there was a rumbling behind us and a Land Rover came bumping down the bank and stopped a few yards away. A young bloke in a T-shirt and shorts climbed out.

"You'll never get rich that way, mate," he said to Terry.

Cheerful enough he was. But that was the wrong thing to say right then. I thought Terry was going to thump him, in spite of all he'd said about aggression.

"Who's trying to get rich?" he bawled out, to the pair of us.

"I am," the young bloke said.

"And I suppose you know a better way than this?" — starting to get confused now, the way he usually did.

"Too right."

With that, the bloke slid this heavy-looking contraption out of the Land Rover, linked it up to the drive, and hauled a long hose down to the water's edge.

"What you got there?" Terry said.

"This? This here's a suction pump. Can collect more gold in an hour than ten men with pans in a day. You see that motor up there? Well . . ."

But Terry wasn't interested in technical explanations. He turned to me with an agonized expression on his face.

"Bloody marvellous, isn't it," he said. "They're not satisfied with ruining the towns. They've got to bring their machines and their mass production methods into the bush. Stuff that up as well. Professional land rapers every one of them. Another example of your modern aggression. Bugger the rivers. Bugger the rights of the individual. Bugger the way of life. Get rich quick at any price, that's all that matters."

"Oh, this won't get me rich," the young bloke said, hoovering all round Terry's feet, damn near sucking the gravel out of the pan. "This is chicken feed, just the preliminaries. Wait until I get into the deep pools. Then you'll see something."

"What? Gold?" said Terry sarcastically. "You wouldn't know real gold if you saw it."

"Oh wouldn't I? Just give me a chance."

Swinging that hose round absent-mindedly and accidentally swallowing up the little glass bottle Terry was collecting the dust in. That does it, I thought, here we go again. But in fact Terry was amazingly well controlled — for him.

"All right," he said, "try this on for size." Whipping open his fly and directing a jet of bright yellow pee straight at the mouth of the hose. "Is that gold enough for you?"

"Hey!" the bloke yelled. "Don't put that muck through my machine!"

"Muck!" Terry shouted, genuinely outraged. "That stuff's too good for your bloody machine. It bears the human touch. Something you wouldn't know anything about. If you weren't so ignorant, you'd realize it's the biggest strike you've ever made."

And with that he picked up his pan and stomped off.

I was fairly keen to stick around and watch for a while. But when Terry's in that mood there's no knowing what he might do. So I reeled in my line and hurried after him.

He was still mumbling and cursing when I caught up. Carrying on about land rapers and somehow managing to bring even the extermination of the wolves in Alaska into his general complaint. I didn't say anything, thinking he'd simmer down, given time. But as chance would have it, when we reached the bridge, there was an old man down in the shallows working a small homemade sluice. Well that only added fuel to the blaze.

"Enjoy it while you can, grandad," Terry called out, "while there's still a few ounces to be had."

"Oh there's plenty left in this river," the old boy replied, "enough to see me out."

"D'you hear that?" Terry said, turning to me, his little eyes blazing. "That's the kind of simple faith this country was built on — which that bastard down there is bent on destroying. Too bloody greedy to leave a few pennyweight for an old man."

I shrugged.

"It can't be helped, Terry," I said.

"Oh can't it? We'll see about that!"

And he turned and charged off down the river.

There was no one in sight when we got back. The Land Rover had been reversed half-way down the bank, close to one of the deep pools; and it was only when we were right up to it that we saw the young bloke — in all his scuba gear at the bottom of the pool, hoovering for all he was worth.

"Look at him!" Terry said contemptuously. "Thinks he's a bloody fish or something."

As he said that, it happened that I really did see a fish. It looked like a big carp. Frightened by the diver, it shot out of the pool and up river. Not too far though. From where I stood I could still see it, about thirty yards away.

"Now don't do anything silly, will you, Terry," I said, starting to pull out some line.

"What, me?" he said. "Next to you two aggressive bastards, I don't even count. Go on, don't worry about me. Get up there and add to the general destruction. Might as well strip the river of fish as well while we're about it."

I could tell he was really angry again, but I still had my eye on that big shadowy outline beneath the surface.

"Have it your own way," I said, and off I went.

The first two casts were a fraction on the short side. But on the third try the line landed just ahead of him, and as the hook floated down, bang, he had it.

"Terry!" I called out. "He's on! Watch him go!"

I glanced over my shoulder, hoping for a bit of applause — only to see the Land Rover slowly inching its way down the bank.

"The Land Rover, Terry!" I yelled. "Look at it!"

He was sitting on a bulge of rock, higher up the bank, in the shadow of an old river oak, grinning all over his face.

"Looks all right to me," he said.

"For God's sake, stop it! Stick a rock under its wheels or something."

"If you're so worried about it, why don't you do it yourself" — still sitting there grinning away, relaxed as you please.

"But I'll lose the fish!"

"Precisely my point all along," he said, chuckling to himself — and I could see nothing was going to shift him.

I really had a bad moment or two there. Those wheels crunching slowly on the gravel and the fish pulling frantically at the end of the line. It was only the thought of the possible consequences which finally decided me, and throwing down the rod I dashed to the rescue.

I was too late though. The back wheels were already in the river, and as I reached for the door they tipped over the edge of the pool and the whole lot went sliding slowly in.

"You're going to kill him!" I shrieked — because the diver was directly underneath the vehicle.

He would have done too. But fortunately the air in the Land Rover stopped it sinking straight off. It hung there for a few seconds in a froth of escaping bubbles, and that gave the diver long enough to clear out. I saw this blank mask staring up at me, and then he shot clear, exactly the way the fish had done earlier.

When he hit the surface, I swear his face was as white as any fish's belly.

"What's going on?" he spluttered, all bewildered.

"That," said Terry, from his throne up on the bank, "was a classic case of the mechanical robot turning on its master. Shades of things to come."

But the young bloke had collected himself a bit by then.

"Who did it?" he said accusingly.

"You couldn't have put the hand brake on, mate," Terry answered, making triumphant swirling actions with his pan.

"You let if off, didn't you?" the young bloke nearly screamed, the truth slowly dawning on him.

"Don't blame me for your mechanical failures," Terry said. "Me, I rely on the human hand." Still swirling the pan and then peering close at it. "What's this I see? A fish? A fish in me bloody pan? Who would have believed it?" Breaking into a great roar of laughter.

But in spite of all his clowning, I noticed he was edging his way along the bank, ready to make his getaway. The young bloke noticed it too.

"Hey," he said, splashing his way towards the shore, "I want your name and address."

"Name and address?" Terry called back, putting the pan on his head as though it was a crown and sort of looking down his nose. "King of the gold fields to you. Care of the Gwydir River."

And he was off down stream.

With all those thousands of dollars worth of gear sunk in eight feet of water, I didn't hang about either. Reeling in my line (no fish, of course), I was off after him.

He put on a fairly cracking pace, in spite of his belly wobbling out there in front of him. But now he was in a great mood.

"Keep it up, grandad," he called out at the bridge. "Plenty of kicks left in the old river yet."

Heaving himself into the front seat of the van and drumming contentedly on the upholstery with dirty fingernails. As soon as we reached the house, he ferreted around in the back and came up with a bottle of whisky.

"I thought you'd destroyed all those bottles," I said, puzzled.

"Ah, I just kept one back. In case we needed to celebrate."

One of his sly chuckles, while he wrestled with the stopper that wouldn't come undone.

"Celebrate?" I said. "What is there to celebrate? All you did was ruin thousands of dollars of equipment and risk the life of an innocent party. Not to mention my fish."

"You're right there," he said, digging me in the ribs. "We lost the tiddler, but we got the big one."

More sly laughter. But puffing now as he continued to pull and twist at the stopper.

"Well don't expect any support from me if he catches

up with you," I said. "As far as I'm concerned, that was a wanton piece of aggression."

"Aggression be buggered!" he said, smashing the neck off the bottle on the side of the table and pouring himself half a glass of whisky.

"What would you call it then?" I asked.

He took a mouthful of grog and leaned back with a satisfied sigh. The glass balanced on the mound of his belly.

"It's more what you'd call a blow for freedom," he said.

## III

The trip to the coast was Terry's idea. "The way it used to be, in the old days," he said. "Camping on the beach, nights spent out under the stars. Not another bugger in sight. No pollution or development. Just us and the sea and sky." Getting so worked up by his own visions of what we were missing that he was out there chucking cans in the back of the van before I could stop him.

It didn't seem too bad an idea at the time. A chance to get away from that slum of his, where you risked your neck whenever you went into the kitchen, having to tip-toe between great piles of dirty dishes.

"You're on," I said, forgetting it was Terry you had to get clear of, not just his house.

To be honest, though, the trip itself started out quite well. Terry was in great spirits. He downed three cans within the first mile or two, and by the time we hit the New England Highway he was leaning out of the side window singing old Bob Dylan numbers to the sheep.

But naturally that couldn't last. Not many miles further on, going through Armidale, we were stopped by a patrol car for speeding. Left to myself, I could probably have talked my way clear. You know, the really humble approach. But just when I was beginning to swing it, Terry had to put in his three cents' worth.

"Oi!" he bawled out. "You in the uniform! You seem to be forgetting you're just a public servant! Why don't you try protecting the public for a change, instead of victimizing it all the time."

The cop hadn't really noticed Terry until then. Now he leaned against the door and bent down, peering inside.

"And get your paws off the bloody car!" Terry added. "You may think you own the road, but you certainly don't own the vehicles on it."

A moment of shocked silence after that, and I really thought we were in the shit. We would have been if I hadn't had a brainwave. Before the cop could open his mouth I said to Terry:

"Hey! That's enough from you! One more word and you can get back on the side of the road where I found you!"

Then to the cop, sort of in confidence:

"Sorry about that. He's just some bikie type I picked up outside Uralla."

For the first time the cop had a good look at him.

"Yes, I can see what he is all right," he said.

Which was not surprising, because in that rotten old singlet of his Terry could have passed as a bikie anywhere. A kind of geriatric version.

"D'you want me to kick him out of there for you?" the cop asked, genuinely considerate all of a sudden.

"No, it's all right," I said, becoming the responsible citizen. "If I leave him behind, he'll only go bothering other motorists."

"It's up to you," he said. "But if he gives you any trouble, just get in touch with us" — actually tipping his cap to me as I put the van into gear, the speeding offense forgotten.

For once Terry had the good sense to keep his mouth shut. For a while anyway. Until we were back on the open road. Then he started up again. But not as I'd expected — not angry and waving his arms about. More gloomy and defeated.

"You're right," he said. "There's no point in arguing with those bastards. They're just the heavies. It's the suit-and-tie brigade, who stand behind them giving the orders — they're the ones we're up against."

"You make it sound like a middle class conspiracy," I said, trying to laugh it off.

"That's exactly what it is," he said, nodding his head despondently and tying bits of his beard into granny knots. "There's not a corner of this country where you can be free any more."

"What about here?" I argued, indicating the bush on either side of us. "Isn't this free enough for you?"

"Free!" he said scornfully. "All I can see is dieback. The result of all their bloody supering. Economic man gone mad."

"All right," I conceded, because there wasn't much else I could say, surrounded as we were by dead and dying trees. "But it'll be different at the coast. You'll see."

"Fat chance," he said moodily. "A fucking pipe dream. You can't escape anywhere these days."

He didn't say much after that. Slumped down in the seat sucking miserably on the cans. Refusing even to look at the healthy forest as we skirted the National Park.

"A zoo for trees," was all I could get out of him.

I let that pass, biding my time till we reached the escarpment.

"Here we are, Terry," I said, "our old stamping

ground. D'you remember when we were lads, tramping up here from the coast? Just the two of us with a couple of packs."

That roused him slightly.

"Yes," he said, grinning, "and you unzipped for a quick pee one afternoon and a bit of spear grass spiked you straight in the . . . "

"It wasn't funny," I broke in — which was a bad mistake, because his laughter died away and he slumped down in the seat again.

From then on I couldn't get a peep out of him. Suit yourself, I thought, I'll soon show you what's what; and I drove like crazy down through Bellingen and straight across the plain to the coast.

But I was in for a bit of a shock myself, because Terry wasn't so far off beam this time. All those dozy little towns I'd remembered from the sixties had been given a face job. Urunga, Vaila, Nambucca — every one of them taken over by real estate men, caravan parks, and Christ knows what.

"See what I mean?" Terry crowed, sitting up just long enough to make his point. "Your suit-and-tie brigade again. It's what they call development. Nowhere's safe from them any more. We're under siege."

"Further north, then," I muttered, doing a uie and heading back the way we'd come — only to find it was more of the same. Coffs, Woolgoolga, Grafton, all tarred with the same brush.

"They're not towns any more," Terry said savagely. "They're fucking tourist centres!"

I didn't argue. Partly because the changes didn't worry me as much as they did him. But also because I'm not one to give up too easy. Putting my foot flat, I made for Byron Bay. Not expecting a lot from the town itself, crummy little hole that it is. No, I had something else in mind altogether.

"You can't have forgotten that beach of ours," I said to Terry a while later as we cleared the limit. "Miles of white sand, with only a few crabs and seagulls to litter the place up."

I nearly nailed him that time — for a few minutes it almost seemed as though I was right. We'd turned off the road, bumped down the track for a while, and there it was. Our old beach, just as we remembered it.

"This is more like it," Terry said, staggering away from the front seat where he'd been crumpled up for the past few hours.

It was fairly late in the afternoon by then, the sun beginning to sink behind the hills, the sea all blue and gold. Bloody marvellous. But we'd no sooner stretched out on the sand than I swear to God this bloody cop materialized out of thin air. A young boy in blue, but with a belly nearly as big as Terry's — which is a damning enough thing to say of anybody.

"I hope you're not planning to spend the night here," he said in his best officialese.

I could see Terry's face start to go red and I quickly grabbed him by one of the saggy loops of his singlet and dragged him back to the van.

"No, officer," I said over my shoulder, "just admiring the view."

Already with the van in gear, reversing it before the cop could say another word.

Thankfully, Terry calmed down pretty quick.

"I should have guessed," he said. "It was too good to be true."

He didn't even complain about the place where we finally spent the night. A side road back in the hills near Main Arm, with mosquitoes coming out of the lantana in squadrons. Some of them so big they nearly carried us off.

"What do you expect," Terry said in the course of the night, when I leaped up for the umpteenth time, my hands and forehead covered with swellings. "At least it's a bloody sight closer to nature than anything you'll find back at the coast."

By dawn he was up flattening the rest of the cans, ready to beat a retreat.

But I still wasn't very keen on admitting I'd been beaten.

"There must be somewhere around here that hasn't been ruined," I said doggedly.

"You reckon," he said cynically. "Go on then. Waste your bloody time if you want to."

Sagging down in the front seat. Picking his nose now there were no cans left.

"Leave your nose alone, Terry!" I snapped at him.

"It steadies me," he said, excavating away, "helps me think."

Well, I don't know about that, but suddenly I had this great idea.

"Wait a minute!" I said. "What day is it?"

"Saturday," he mumbled, not really interested.

"Then that's it! We've been looking in the wrong place. We should be up round Lismore or Kyogle way. It's at the weekends they have those people's markets."

"So what?" Terry said.

"So that's where we'll find the real people. The unspoiled scene."

I said it with as much enthusiasm as I could muster, because frankly I'm not keen on all that shaking of tambourines and clean living stuff. I just thought it would get Terry out of the doldrums and kind of save my own face, if you see what I mean.

He didn't exactly brim over with joy at the suggestion, but he did hesitate slightly.

"It could be worth a try . . . " he said uncertainly.

That was good enough for me.

"Bloody oath!" I said.

And before he could change his mind, I was off, belting along those crummy back roads that shook and jolted the old van until our teeth rattled.

As a trip, it was no fun, I can tell you. And after all that trouble it achieved precisely nothing. Oh, we found our people's market all right. But so had three zillion holiday makers, the coaches that had brought them surrounding the group of stalls like an urban stockyard. And there, in amongst the stalls themselves, the full tourist invasion: cameras thick as flies on a steer's arse; walk-shorts stretched around over-fed guts; blue rinses on shaky old skulls. All dead set on witnessing the joys of the alternative life style.

"Jesus Christ!" Terry screamed out, as we drew up between two buses. "They've taken over! Every man for himself!"

"Steady on," I said, trying to calm him. "It's not as bad as it looks."

"Isn't it?" he said. "How bad's it going to look when it's really bad?"

"Well, I mean . . . " I said, scratching around for ideas, "there're the locals, the ones running the stalls. Aren't they your kind of people?"

I realized straight off I shouldn't have said that. His face went red again and I thought he was going to choke.

"People!" he finally exploded. "Is that what you call them! Don't be fooled by the long hair and head bands. They're just professional rip-off artists living off the backs of tourism."

I shrugged helplessly.

"So what do we do now?" I said.

"Do? We get the hell out of here. Back home where we can at least lock the door."

I reached for the ignition key. But right then there was this roar of engines and half a dozen bikies came gunning down the road. A really prize bunch. Wearing the usual collection of chains and nazi helmets, and with their ragged denims and bare skin caked with dirt and grease. Even Terry looked fairly respectable next to that lot. The leader of the group, I remember, had tattooed down one arm, "I GOT SYPHILIS". And when he stepped off his bike the tourists scattered in all directions.

"You're right," I said, "we'd better make tracks out of here."

But Terry reached over and stopped me. Genuinely cheerful at last. The brightest he'd been since the cop had waved us over back in Armidale.

"Hang on," he said, eyeing the bikies and grinning, "this is more like it."

"Like what?" I said. "All I can see is trouble."

"Yes, trouble for the tourists," he said, chortling happily to himself as the bikies sauntered towards the stalls, knocking little old ladies out of the way and kicking a couple of shiny airline bags into the dust.

"Did you see that?" he said, chuckling and bouncing up and down on the seat. "That'll teach the bastards."

But the best was still to come as far as Terry was concerned. As the bikies passed one of the buses, the leader opened his fly and peed down its side. A thin yellow stream cutting a curved path through the dust covering the white paintwork.

Terry was absolutely beside himself.

"Attaboy Syphilis!" he crowed, and started to wind down the window, obviously intending to yell out encouragement.

"For Christ's sake, Terry!" I said, dragging him away from the window. "You'll have them on our backs in a minute!"

"Them?" he said, looking at me as though I had a screw loose or something. "You've got it all wrong, mate. The bikies are on our side — against that suit-and-tie brigade out there."

"What are you talking about, Terry? That's just a crowd of middle-aged tourists. I can't see any suits and ties."

"They're on holiday, damnit!" Terry said, but still grinning as Syphilis crunched his boot down on some sun glasses dropped by a nervous old pair of walk-shorts.

"Please yourself," I said, "but I'm clearing out while I've got the chance."

Again I reached for the ignition. But it was just like the first time. Before I could turn the key, there was another roar of engines and a few of the bikies' mates rode up. They were more or less like the others, except that one of them had a loose furry shape draped over his petrol tank.

"What's that?" Terry said suspiciously.

I wasn't sure. Not until the bikie heaved it off the tank and dragged it after him. Then I saw it was a dead dog. A spaniel, I think. Probably one he'd just run over, because the body left a trail of fresh-looking blood on the ground.

"What the fucking hell's he up to?" Terry said — not grinning now.

We soon found out. The bikie with the dog tossed it up about shoulder high, and several others, including Syphilis, grabbed hold of a leg each. Just as though they were at a Colonel Sanders barbecue. Then, with a couple of powerful jerks, they tore the body apart.

"Hey!" Terry said, "that's not funny" — edging forward on his seat.

"What are you worrying about?" I said. "They're one of us. You told me so."

"No," he murmured, really concerned. "Human beings are one thing. But animals! That's different. Different thing altogether."

The bikies hadn't finished yet though. While Terry was busy murmuring, his old mate Syphilis raised the torn-off leg he was holding, still with a long string of bluish-red gut clinging to it, and began eating the raw flesh. Right there, in front of everyone. The fresh blood running down his stubbly chin and dripping between his feet.

"Jesus fucking Christ!" Terry said, and before I could stop him he was half out of the van.

"What do you think you're doing?" I said, trying to grab him.

But he shook me off.

"You can either give me a hand or shut up," he said, and he slammed the door.

Well, put like that, it wasn't a difficult choice to make. So I rolled the windows closed and locked both doors.

Fortunately I don't think Terry even noticed. Without a backward glance, he strode quickly between the buses and into the market. Shouldering tourists out of his way as though he was hardly aware of them. There were still quite a few around, as you can imagine. Enjoying the fun. But not Terry. He went straight up to Syphilis, snatched the leg out of his hands, and put it gently down on one of the stalls. I noticed that particularly, how gently he did it.

He never had a chance to straighten up. While he was still bent forward, Syphilis kicked him in the mouth and down he went. The others soon climbed in. A whole circle putting the boot into poor old Terry.

There was nothing anybody could do but watch. So

for a minute or two I joined the tourists. It may even have been longer, because I didn't get out of the van and go over to him until the bikies had ridden off.

I wouldn't have been surprised to find him dead. As it was, he was a shocking mess. His front teeth all kicked in. His lips and eyebrows split. So much blood on the front of his singlet that you couldn't see the gravy stains.

"My God, Terry!" I said, bending over him.

But he was a tough bastard, I'll give him that.

"Pfuggin parshtars," he said, mumbling through the blood that filled his mouth, and hauling himself up onto his knees.

"Here, hang on to me," I said.

With one of his arms round my neck, I half-helped, half-dragged him over to the van — but not before some little old lady had taken a sly snap of him with her instamatic.

Sprawled out in the front seat he looked even worse. Really showing his years. And I didn't know what to do for a while. But there was a box of tissues under the dashboard and I used a bundle of those to wipe most of the gore away. Surprisingly, once he'd cleared his mouth of blood and bits of broken tooth, he could speak quite clearly.

"Someone had to show them," he said, breathing heavily.

"You're right there, Terry," I answered.

Dabbing at his poor buggered mouth with a wad of tissues and wishing I was back in Newcastle, away from all this.

"Everyone's got to make a stand sometime," he added, running his tongue along the split in his lip, speaking more to himself than to me. "The problem is knowing whose side you're really on."

"Nobody doubts your loyalty, Terry," I said, "not after that."

Trying to cheer him up.

But he was perkier than I thought. Suddenly looking at me with a little of the old twinkle in his one good eye and holding his hand up to his gashed mouth to stop himself laughing.

"Just the same," he said ruefully, "it's a fucking dog's life. Isn't it?"

# Reflections

Infirm though he is, he has a very particular view of his own situation. The house itself he thinks of as quaint. A narrow terrace which he vaguely locates in one of the more fashionable inner suburbs of Sydney. He doesn't care to be more definite than that. Yet in his mind's eye he can see the exterior clearly enough: a beautifully restored facade; the verandahs festooned with traditional lace work; the narrow strip of garden, behind the black iron railings, overflowing with bougainvillaea and the dark glossy leaves of rubber plant. He, the author of this picture, is always a central feature of it. An old man, brown and wiry, still supple-limbed, relaxing in a cane chair on the lower verandah. His feet, in well cobbled leather shoes, are resting on the painted balustrade, his silky white hair falling gracefully over his left temple, the air about him redolent with the rich aroma of pipe tobacco. He is, to all appearances, an old man at peace with the world, gazing out onto a street undisturbed by motorized traffic. Only pedestrians pass his door — always well dressed, unhurried, glancing up at him, enviously perhaps, as they saunter by.

That, in essence, is how he visualizes it all. His mind leaping the walls, the public thoroughfare, the immediate sensation, to gaze back from the hazy blue which is all that remains of the opposite side of the street.

He, meanwhile, lies quietly in the back upstairs room of the house. Here the walls are dirty and discoloured, much of the plaster cracked or fallen away, revealing the rough brickwork beneath. Across the single window hangs a yellowed scrap of nylon curtain. Above his head, as though in sympathy with the bed beneath, the ceiling sags dangerously. His thin, bony frame creates no more than a ripple in the grey blanket covering him; and his hands, heavy veined, resting on his chest, appear unnaturally large. The swollen, distorted finger joints are oddly in keeping with the face which is horribly disfigured. He can still recall, if he cares to, the cancerous sore inside his mouth, the metallic taste of it on the tip of his tongue. That at least is gone. As is his right ear. One whole side of his face shiny with scar tissue. His mouth — pulled out of shape, thrust over to the space where his cheek should have been — now little more than a functional wound, small and round and strained open in perpetual readiness.

He lies like this, quiet and alone, for more than an hour before the silence is disturbed. Then the front door opens and he hears footsteps on the stairs. He is aware of who it is without needing to look. The light, quick tread as familiar to him, or so it seems, as his own life history. This one identical to every other. All of them indistinguishable, coming to him for the same reason; a stream of young girls, one after the other, day after day, seeking his advice. Not begging him. Always reticent, shy — hiding their embarrassment behind a pretense of busying themselves about the room. But he knows what they want just the same, what they're really here for. A lifetime's wisdom distilled into a few well chosen words. Not welcome news to them, perhaps, running counter to their romantic longings, but true for all that. The truth as he has lived it, fashioned it; as certain, as incontrovertible, as his dream image of the house.

She enters the room and he chuckles softly, knowingly, to himself, his head moving restlessly from side to side on the pillow. The scar-strained opening on the edge of his face changes shape slightly as he tries to speak.

"... about being old," he tells her, the words blurred, broken, yet perfectly clear to himself: "... one good thing... no need to pretend... not any more... Only the young tell lies... We're the ones... we know..."

She shows no signs of having heard. Intent now on lifting him, turning him, smoothing out the sheet beneath his wrinkled back; and later washing the emaciated torso and limbs with swabs of cotton wool. Saying nothing as she works. Handling him as she would a corpse or some mummified form which has lost all power to impinge upon her. Later still, when the door bell rings, she brings the hot dishes upstairs and feeds him. Sitting beside the bed, as silent and unresponsive as before, gazing out through the soiled curtain while she absently spoons the food through the hole in his face.

While she works he continues to talk. The words streaming through his mind in a clear undeniable current of sound which, for him, has little or no connection with the barely audible mixture of grunts and groans which issue out into the room. That other noise, he considers, is no concern of his, of no more importance than the ticking of the clock on the shelf. Mindless of the mush of food which trickles down his chin, staining the collar of his pyjamas, he concentrates on polishing each phrase. Getting it exactly right. So perfect that the past will be powerless to mar it in any way.

"The love thing..." he croaks out, "... a con... number one... that's all... no other nonsense... and marriage... two bodies in a house... just two bodies... I made that plain to her... here in this room ... night after night... that's what kept her happy... nothing else..."

Momentarily he sees, as through a darkened window, an image of a woman facing him: kneeling on the bed, legs splayed, dressed only in a faded slip. She is crying and her mouth is open wide, twisted oddly sideways as she screams soundlessly. He has not conjured this picture. It is simply there, rising slowly within him, and he forces it back down into the darkness as he would an unwelcome belch.

"This . . . " he says, his own ruined mouth strangely mirroring her agonized expression, " . . . it's all there is . . . joining us . . . till death do us . . . and she knew . . . same as I did . . . when she was well off . . . wanting the same as me . . . underneath . . . underneath it all . . . all any of them . . . all the same . . . "

The stream of incoherent sound continues as the hours pass. From time to time, whenever he refers to her, this unknown woman of the past who first twisted her face into this likeness of his, he tastes yet again the cancerous sore (acid, corrosive) which once bloomed, blossomed, inside his mouth, an obstacle which sought to balk the enunciated passage of the truth he has come to live by. But this too he dismisses, murmuring, " . . . tongued her . . . tongued her . . . ", the words like an incantation which instantly dispels all immediate sensation, returning him to this closed and empty room of the present.

Only once in the course of the day is the current of his thought seriously diverted. There is a muffled sound from the far side of the room. Two figures embracing or struggling in the doorway. The old man turns and half raises his head: sees and actually recognizes one of them. The taller, heavier one.

"My grandson . . . " he says with a flicker of pride, somehow mustering the effort to make the words intelligible.

Neither figure responds, the embrace or struggle continuing. A surge of envy, hatred, mists his sight, and he snarls out, still with a semblance of clarity:

"Not like me... you couldn't... not like me... the way I held her... whether she liked it or not... and she did... did..."

There is a savage rejoinder from the dark, struggling figure, followed by a whispered plea, half-hearted, uncertain. But he is oblivious once more, totally alone in the space he has chosen for himself. His mottled tongue probing, probing, at the unknown cave of his own mouth. Moistening the livid, strained oval of skin that serves him for lips. His mind lifting him free of the temptations of sound or taste. Ministering to him more assiduously than this girl (or any of those who came before her) could have thought possible. Whirling the afternoon past him in a phantasm of colour which settles at last into the brooding, threatening quality of a dusk he cannot deny. The ignored, forgotten side of this street on which he has always lived rising in ruins through the haze of blue.

She, too, has grown accustomed to these daily visits. It makes little difference to her where she goes or to whom. On this particular morning she duplicates the route she has taken for some weeks now, both seeing and not seeing the poor Newtown area through which she walks, pacing quickly, efficiently along a street lined on two sides by shabby, often sordid terraced housing; stopping at last and entering a broken-down relic of the past, its narrow sagging verandahs closed in by fibro sheeting interspersed with small, dirty window panes. Once inside, she returns the key to her bag and mounts the creaking stairs, her starched skirt rustling against her thighs.

The old man is where he always is, laid out on the bed, his head thrown back in the similitude of death. She gives him no greeting. Accords him the merest glance. His mumbled speech, which she has never understood, flowing past her unnoticed. She is all efficiency, doing only and precisely what she has been sent here for. A young woman, considerably less than thirty, with a face not so much unhappy as unnaturally impassive, going diligently about her duties, ministering to this body which claims her attention rather than her care.

In some ways she is a peculiar match for the old man. Neither of them able to force a passage through the dark confines of memory; both equally obsessed by the chosen shape of previous events. Time conceived neither as a flowering nor as a process of decay. Each successive day caught up in the same tight circle which feeds upon itself, which allows no intrusion from without.

This day is as yet no exception. As she works, heaving the body up and over, washing it, tending it, she contemplates a vague kaleidoscope of images which have come to dog her waking hours. Which already threaten to become the touchstones of her young experience. There is nothing startling about these half imagined scenes. Typical amongst them is a vision of herself kneeling naked on an unmade bed, her lips parted by an emotion she cannot read. In others no less typical she is lying with pale legs raised above her head, a wash of sweat across her breasts, her voice, harsh and urgent, crying out for something she has no words to articulate — a knowledge or a feeling that slips beyond her reach with the shudder of the moment.

In all such images no other person is present except herself. Only the shadow of another. Something indefinably male hovering at the very edge of consciousness, vague and indistinct, imbued with a lingering aura of romance. A suggestive outline rather than a real person, an almost ghostly presence which she both acknowledges and desires with an inchoate sense of unease.

Not perhaps without reason. Because in the early afternoon this indistinct, shadowy figure takes on concrete shape. As she knows it always must, eventually. She hears the bolt of the front door drawn back; his heavy footsteps on the stairs. Mounting. It is not even the first time he has appeared, pushing his way into the back bedroom as he has done before. But suddenly more open in his intentions.

"Hush," she says, feigning concern, "we mustn't disturb him."

He waves his hand carelessly.

"He's had his turn," he says, "it's ours now."

Behind them, the mumbled speech drones on.

"But here!" she replies, "here!"

Allowing that one word to express all her vague misgivings about this and every other such encounter.

"What does it matter?" he objects. "Here or anywhere, it comes to the same thing."

"But I wanted . . ." she begins, "I . . ."

For answer he compels her towards him, kisses her with parted lips. She tastes the inside of his mouth, the sharp metallic edge to it. Which repels and attracts her simultaneously. As does the way he draws up her skirt, thrusting at her unashamedly.

With difficulty she pulls away. And at that moment the old invalid in the corner raises his head and calls out to them. The sound means nothing to her, but the young man, unexpectedly perturbed by the interruption, turns savagely towards the bed.

"Listen to him!" he jeers. "As if he had room to talk. The way she walked out and left him."

"No . . ." she objects uncertainly.

"But I tell you she did," he insists, "the old lady. Thirty or more years ago. Just walked out. If you ask me he probably couldn't get it up. Went dry on her."

He swivels round and smiles confidently. A smile curiously without promise.

"You'll never have that problem with me," he assures her, reaching out once again.

But a lingering sense of unease makes her hesitate. Even when he forces her against the door, jamming his knee suggestively between her legs.

"What's the matter?" he demands.

"Give me time," she stammers out.

He steps away, affronted.

"What are you after?" he says accusingly.

"Nothing..." she says. "A bit more time... that's all."

Which she recognizes, with regret, is nothing less than the truth.

"You think time will make anything different?" he says, his voice raised against her. "You're not a kid any longer. You know the score."

That, at least, she cannot deny. But still some instinct prompts her to fend him off, if only temporarily.

"Time..." she whispers.

Her hands push at his chest, stubbornly rejecting him despite her inability to think of anything other than the sensation of his mouth fumbling for hers; the hot, sharp touch of cheek and tongue; the sheer naked taste.

It is that sensation which continues to occupy her thoughts long after he has gone and the storm of his departing protest has died away. A confused animal flavour which inspires in her both desire and uneasiness. An elusive quality which makes her scrub her hand across her mouth, as though wiping something away, and only moments later furtively savour the alien taint that lingers not only on her lips and tongue, but seems to permeate the very atmosphere of the room. Growing stronger, if that is possible, enveloping her the more, as the day advances and the first suggestion of impending dusk seeps into the deathly stillness of the waiting house.

In the early evening, her silent vigil over, she departs the house without so much as a backward glance. At the closing of the door, the old man, with whom she has nominally spent the day, ceases to exist for her; what little reality he may have had throughout the daylight hours dissolving instantly in the impersonal spaces of the shadow-streaked street. During the long journey home — walking quickly along the shabby thoroughfares of Newtown, and later sitting straight and still in the crowded bus — it never occurs to her that she might spare him a moment's consideration. Only once, in fact, and then involuntarily, is her memory of him faintly stirred.

She is climbing slowly up the narrow stairs towards her third floor flat. Just as she reaches the second landing, the door on her left opens and an old, bent figure darts out and tries to bar her way. As on other occasions, she flinches aside, repelled by the almost overpowering odour of unwashed skin and clothes which emanates from the flat as well as from the man himself.

"Hello, dearie," he says, and tries to rub himself against her, his wizened, elfin-like face peering up at her from under abundant, grey-streaked eyebrows.

"Keep away from me!" she says threateningly. "I've warned you before."

"That's what she always told me," he replies defiantly, but he moves away slightly, back in the direction of the open door.

She sidles past him and he leers at her sadly, the

expression pulling his mouth sideways. And it is then that she recalls the old invalid in the distant house. It is, in a vaguely literal sense, her last encounter with the living man, because only seconds later, unseen by her or anyone, completely alone in the deepening dusk, with even the grimy window reduced to a blue-black square facing ineffectually out onto the encroaching night, he takes a last deep, searching breath and dies.

At that precise moment she is placing the key in the empty lock. No intimation of his passing reaches her across the bustling city. No touch of chill makes her pause and consider. She has already forgotten him. His thin insubstantial image replaced by the more potent image of the grandson. His full, searching mouth reaching out towards her.

On this particular evening she doesn't switch on the light. She is happier in the darkened room. Tomorrow, she decides, he will visit her again. And then . . . There is no need to flesh out a reality she understands only too well. It will follow its own familiar course. Nothing she can say or do will deflect it. But in the meantime, during this brief period of respite, she sits in the darkness that, unwittingly, she has come to share with the old man, and imagines other possibilities — this room, with its all too suggestive shadows, magically transported beyond the confines of a harsh, gaunt house; mellowed and softened to the point where he, unbidden, will silently enter a totally other darkness; one in which she will wait, expectant, at ease, made confident by the unviolated space that separates them; a space that only she, uncoerced, can bridge.

She is roused from such dreams by the sudden opening of the door. Startled, she looks up and recognizes, in the light spilling in from the passage, the small figure of the child who lives in the first floor flat.

"Nurse!" he calls out, unable to see her in the

darkness, "Nurse! You're wanted on the phone."

"I'm coming," she says resignedly, rising and smoothing out her rumpled skirt, already convinced of what she must expect. Ready, in spite of herself, to acquiesce.

But when she reaches the lower passageway and lifts the receiver to her ear, she is surprised to discover that it is someone from the nursing service. The voice, like a minister of the night itself, informs her of her patient's sudden death in clipped impersonal tones. She nods, taking in the simple fact, and then, with unconscious irony, she writes in the curve of her palm the address of her next assignment.

It is that address alone which occupies her as she turns once more towards the stairs — only to find her way barred, for the second time that evening, by the gnome-like figure of the man who occupies the second floor flat. He winks at her, nods knowingly, and again gives her that suggestive leer which momentarily disfigures his face.

"You're not like her," he says, "not a bit. No one is. She was . . . she was . . . "

Unable to find the exact word, he raises one arm in a vague gesture and a foul waft of stale sweat and dirt strikes her full in the face. Not for the first time she notices how obviously unwashed he is: his clothes stiff with grease; his skin brackish and discoloured with ingrained grime.

Trying to control her spontaneous feeling of repugnance, she says:

"Will you let me pass, please?"

He seems not to hear her, his slightly crazed eyes wavering past her face.

"That's why I've never remarried," he continues, just as though she hasn't spoken. "You're not lucky twice, not in this life. It was better to preserve her. That was what I decided."

"Preserve her?" she says, intrigued despite her desire to escape.

"Keep her always," he says, "here," and he points to the bare skin of his own hand.

"I don't think I understand..." she says uncertainly.

"The smell of her, here," he explains, "never washed off. The taste of her, the way she was."

He raises his hand and licks his own palm. Lovingly. With a show of tenderness which affronts her. His lips parting to mouth gently at the unwashed flesh.

"Sweet," he says, "sweet. Like her."

Tears, like rheum, showing in his eyes.

"Stop it!" she bursts out. "Don't be disgusting!"

She pushes past him, shouldering him roughly aside, and hurries up the narrow stairwell.

But once within the safety of her own room, she discovers, with reluctance, that it is not disgust which has moved her. Sweet, he called it, the clean, unspoiled pink of tongue and lip showing unmistakably as he sought for her memory. Sweet. A wash of tears threatening to course down the grimy cheeks. Sweet.

She stirs uneasily in the darkness. For the reiteration of that one word has reminded her of another mouth. Closing on her own. The sharp taste of it, acid and corrosive. The full lips, where they meet hers, withering, growing thin; the whole mouth twisting to one side until, to her horror, she finds that she is kissing the gaping wound in the cheek of the old man.

She stand up, clicks on the overhead light, and walks quickly over to the window. The glass pane, uncurtained, clearly reflects her own likeness back at her. But it is not herself whom she sees. For the first time she is looking at the face of the old man. Really seeing him at last. The terrible disfigurement which the years have wrought; time, like some corrosive substance, eating away at the passive flesh; the features ruined and warped by forces he has failed to control; the mouth, above all, horribly violated. Almost as if some special judgment, a curse perhaps, has descended upon it.

That thought, once evoked, will not be stilled. A judgment. And unable to deny it access, she too begins to cry. Quietly. To herself. Without realizing it, she is grieving for the old man. Hers the only tears that will be shed for him either on this night or in the days that are to follow. A silent keening he is oblivious of, that in all likelihood he would have scorned. A grief that she also finds unwelcome. Her eyes tight closed against her own sorrow, against this image of herself, still clearly reflected in the window, which faces in towards her from the outer darkness.